THE SENATOR'S DAUGHTER

INFINITE TENDERNESS SERIES

MARGAUX FOX

1
LOLA

The club hides its secrets in the thick, dark air. Fluorescent lights mark out the stage and the neon strobes flicker to a beat of their own. The throb of bass pulses through the air and liquor is poured in ample measures. Welcome to . . . McLandon's. The sign sits a little tilted at the back of the bar and the neon has dulled over the years, but it still hums throughout all hours of the day and night. Time loses its meaning the second you walk through the doors, and that's just how it should be--temptation wrapped in a pretty, dark bow.

The lights drop as I stroll out down the walkway. Dark aviators cover my eyes, shielding them from the neon that flickers across my skin. My hair is short, in a bright pink bob, and my lips are glossy and full. I take each step casually, balancing perfectly in my high, glass-like heels. My body can barely be seen, hidden in the darkness as I make my way to the very front, walking high above, looking over my shades as I catch eyes and answer with a wink.

I nod to the back and the UV light suddenly flashes across my skin. My underwear lights up, glowing bright against my body. The neon green gleams, catching the light with every roll of my hips. The lace kisses my chest, the material light, letting my breasts bounce as I dance slowly, putting on the show people came to see.

I raise my hands high up above my head, my fingers threading as I spin on one heel. The neon lace riding high against the curve of my ass gives the audience a perfect view of my ripe, peachy cheek. Facing the back, I turn, glancing over my shoulder, my teeth running along my lower lip before I bite down. I give my cheek a soft slap, making ripples vibrate along my curves.

Lowering and turning in a half circle, my knees bend outwards wide, my ass hovering a few inches from the floor, the muscles in my thighs tight and toned as I spread. That flashing UV light brings gazes to the pulsing green between my legs. My pussy is lit up as the lights bathe her in a neon glow.

My fingers rest against the tender skin of my ankle bone. I slowly begin to stand, my fingertips tracing up my body. They trail along my inner thighs, turning out to glide over lace, running against my sides before following the curve of my spine. With an expert flick, my nails catch the clasp of my bra and my breasts are freed with a tiny bounce. I slip the straps from my shoulders, baring my full, pert breasts.

Reaching to the side of the stage, I dip my hands in thick, creamy neon paint. I place my palms flat on my stomach and slide up, smearing neon trails over my ribs before I cup my breasts, rolling my nipple seductively slow between my fingers and thumbs. They harden under my touch, the paint cool and bright against my creamy skin, lighting me up in a fluorescent glow.

I reach for more paint and it drips from my fingers, splashing along my thighs, leaving creamy, neon strands. My wet fingers start on my hips, slipping under my panties. Paint dribbles from the sopping lace as I cup my pussy under the fabric. I roll my neck back, my fake, short bob bouncing as I moan. . . . The UV light flickers off and my body plunges into darkness.

It is one of my messier shows, which means more clean-up time after. The janitor gets really pissy with me if I get excess paint on the stage. But the paint gets me the tips. Something about creamy fluids smeared across a nearly naked girl seems to get guys hot under the collar.

But I am careful with the mess. I slide into the backstage area, which for a strip joint is not quite as dingy as one might expect, and start to peel off the perfectly dried neon paint.

The space is minimal, small, organized, and clean--mainly because myself and the other girls have been around a while and we like things to be, you know, not gross.

At the wrong end of my twenties, I really am nearing the age of stripper retirement. I have been on this stage for nearly ten years and at one time, "Lola" was a mask. A part of me I was ashamed of. Now I forget the girl I used to pretend to be. For all the stigma that comes with stripping, there really is a life to be had in the pleasures of the night. And I have found a home here, as unconventional as that may be.

There is a tap on the door and the bossman himself peeks his head around. "You were great out there, Lola. Love that song choice with the neon. Always a favorite." He treats me to a warm smile and I feel him power up the charm offensive. "We have a private party tomorrow. . . . I know you don't usually work, but you were requested. Specifically. Big tips."

"Oh, Landon . . .You certainly know the way to this girl's heart." I grin at him.

If you think of every stereotype you have ever heard about a strip joint owners—that they are old, fat, groping, entitled, that they smoke, and that they are just general assholes—you could throw them all out the window with Landon. He is polite, professional, and sees us as women and definitely not objects. He hires well, takes care of the good ones, and lets the bad go. (The girls on drugs are a problem that just can't be solved in a place like this.)

All the girls crush hard on him. Hell, I even crushed hard on him at one point, and I am very very, very gay. That smile of his could make a heart melt in seconds. I often wondered if it wasn't those big blue eyes of his that made all the panties drop around here. But Landon is mysterious in a way that means we can lust after him, but never touch him, which probably only adds to his allure. He never sleeps with the girls.

"If I knew the way to your heart, Lola, I would be a guy in trouble, but as it stands I will happily fill your pockets with cash." He gives me one last smile before giving the side of the door a little tap, like a knock on wood, which is endearingly charming. "Get home safe," he finishes, before drawing the door closed softly behind him.

I let out a little sigh. He's right; I don't like to work Mondays, but I also don't have plans that can't wait for another day. My hot date with ice cream and watching reruns of Jersey Shore, while alluring, can wait until Tuesday.

"Lola . . ." Chuck calls through the door. "You heading out or you wanna take a private dance in booth three?" I glance at the clock. It's after two but I don't feel tired. These thighs still have some grind left in them.

"Liquor 'em up, Chuck, I will be through in five."

"Got you." I hear him step away as I pull my real hair out from under the synthetic pink bob and run my fingers through the long dark curls.

2

WILLOW

If I roll my eyes any harder, they will be stuck staring at my brain cells--which I'm in real danger of losing while working with this bunch.

"Are we seriously not past the male cliché of strip joints and hookers in 2023?" I ask with a sigh, already knowing the answers I'm about to be showered with.

"Oh, come on, Willow! Don't act like you are better than the strip club. Nothing better than a bourbon, titties, and ass on a Monday night!" Bill hollers from over the booth, as Jim starts throwing out the single dollar bills while making lewd gestures.

"Clichéd and cheap," I say with a sigh, and spin in my swivel chair to gaze at my screen.

I knew I was a little hard on them in some ways. I'm the only woman in here—a token. I am well aware that my hiring had nothing to do with my 4.0 GPA, nor the fact that I graduated summa cum laude from an Ivy League school that I worked my absolute ass off for. Neither was my employment due to my charity donations, volunteer work, nor the fact that I sold my soul to the intern gods. No. It's because of my father that I'm here--but hey, that is a conversation for my therapist.

But the guys have embraced me. I have to give them credit for that. They don't hide who they are or keep me out of the loop. They don't put on airs and graces in case I go running to Daddy. They are cautious around me and make an effort to respect my personal space, giving me work that challenges but doesn't overwhelm me, and they invite me to work events.

Like Monday night strip club outings.

I look down at my dry-cleaned Armani suit. The skirt is perfectly pressed and fitted to me, my stockings have a sheen but are also nearly opaque so they are still office appropriate, and my shirt is tucked to show off my figure. The outfit is designed to give the impression tha I am here to work. I know that I'm put together. It's a well-crafted veneer of perfection that I've spent my entire life creating. And I wasn't sure it would blend too well in tonight's venue. I knew if I went home, I'd talk myself out of going, and if I did that . . . I'm just not sure playing hooky gives the right impression when I am trying to fit in with my male colleagues. Willow Rutherford: The Prude.

On the other hand, I figure I won't really be high on anyone's radar in a strip club as the only woman in a group of balding, middle-aged men who have a lot of cash and are desperate for female attention. I'm guessing the bar will be well-stocked and, overall, it will be an experience. Pretty sure I shouldn't be nearly in my thirties, having never set foot into the dark side of town. So I decide I'll go with them to the strip club.

It's obvious as we reach the entrance who comes here often. Of the group of us, only a couple of the guys make their way straight to the side door, not bothering with the front because they know the reservation procedure. And funnily enough, it's not the ones who talked the big talk. Those macho guys seem a little more unsettled but also excited, which makes me want to be sick in my mouth at the thought of it. This kind of place exploits women, and I can't quite get past that.

The security guy gives me a little smile and a nod, and I wonder about his story. What he might have seen coming in and out of this place. How many women were like me.

McLandon's. Not the worst name for a place like this. At least it wouldn't look too bad on the company account the next day, and you could probably hide your visit from your wife.

I step inside and it takes a second for my eyes to adjust, but then they widen and I feel my eyebrows raising as I drink in the details. Everything is crafted to entice. The stage is raised to the perfect height above the seats so eyes will be drawn up, invited to explore the dancers performing. Mirrored walls offer reflections, glimpses of hidden flesh. Blackened walls, comfortable seats, and the sweep of spotlights make time freeze. The world could be waking outside, but this place seems to live in the eternal, scandalous night. It makes my breath catch in my throat.

I settle at the bar, taking whatever drink is pushed in my direction as my gaze drifts from one scene to the next. It's all so disorienting. Hard to imagine how many people are here, how big the place is, and who is who . . . but I guess that's all part of the narrative. You're supposed to be focused on one thing. As if the whole club is following my thoughts, the lights dim, a silence settles and I can feel the static of anticipation sizzle through the air as she comes into view. For a second my heart stops altogether and only one question lingers on my breathless lips. Who is she?

3
LOLA

Differences hover in the air from last night and the setup is a bit altered, but the atmosphere still tingles, all the same. The buzz of adrenaline. My eyes are already glazed as I lean in for the final swipe of crimson, pupils dilated so my blue irises seem to have darkened to black. I stand slowly, tall on skyscraper heels, barely dressed in slips of silk, and my bronze skin is perfectly oiled . . . . I step out onto a dark stage.

The strobe sweeps over my skin, starting at my ankles and rising up my bare, toned legs as my fingers curl around the polished pole. My knees part, thighs spreading, and my hips dip into a slutty drop. A slither of fabric barely covers my blushing sex. My stomach presses forward and I feel the kiss of cold steel against my skin, as my breasts rest heavily in tied silk on either side of the pole.

My grip closes, red painted fingernails tightening their hold as I begin to writhe, my body following a seductive rhythm as I grind myself against the pole.

I love to dance and know I am an exceptional dancer. My body was created for men to look at and I've made my peace with that. My body is lean in the right places and full, luscious, and curved in others. My waist is narrow and my legs long. I possess a natural elegance that cannot be learned. My lips are full and my blue eyes seductive.

Men want me. They always have.

At first, when I realized this at twelve years old, it was alarming. I didn't want the men in return and in the following years, it became very clear that I was gay.

It didn't matter. I learned to accept that men wanted me--wanted to look at me. So I learned how use that to my advantage. My significant financial advantage.

Now when men gaze at me, they pay for the

privilege. In my opinion, that is exactly how it should be.

Now my body is begging for attention. The attention it so deserves. My body understands as I feel the eyes in the room following me. My head tilts and I sweep my hair around, my natural long dark curls flipping away from my face.

I see a woman in the crowd. Unusual, but not the first time, or, I suspect, the last.

I only catch a glimpse. The intensity of her gaze surprises me. At a glance, the woman looks immaculately put together and expensive. I choose to meet her gaze with my own, giving her a view into my dark soul.

My right thigh rises upward, knee bending as my leg snakes around the pole. My body follows in a seductively salacious curve. My spin is slow and deliberate, my back arching so that my hair trails behind me as I go round and round. My body is much stronger than it looks. As well as hours spent training on the pole, I do weights in the gym. I eat well and look after my body. I take my work seriously. I do everything in my power to be the best I can, and I know it pays off.

My stiletto finds the floor and I stand with my back against the pole. McLandon's is dark as the strobes dim, but then the backlight bursts with life and my frame is displayed as a silhouette. My arms curl upwards, fingers tangling through my curls and then pulling on the string around my neck. The moment the bow unties, my breasts fall with a soft bounce. Fabric falling, discarded, as I bare myself in tiny panties, waiting for dollars to line the floor.

As the spotlights dance over me once again, I feel their heat on my naked skin. My body is their canvas and they paint me as they please. I feel my nipples harden conveniently under their glare, knowing that it adds to my allure. My hands reach up and take hold of the pole above my head as I lower myself. My knees spread outwards, thighs parting as my ass settles just above my heels. I hold myself wide, and open. Almost everything is on display. Almost.

Letting go, I fall forward. My knees find the stage, palms resting against the floor, fingers fanning outward. I crawl toward the front. My eyes are filled with dark temptation because I know I can be exactly what the clients want. And by doing so, I can take their money.

Do you want me to beg for you? I think. My tongue rims my lips as I inch forward. My breasts fall heavy with soft swings and my hips snake, the sway of my ass mirrored around the stage. I am naked except for a small flash of red silk that aches to be torn from me.

I see the woman again and am drawn to her. She is beautiful in a posh business type way.

Focus, Lola.

I pick one of the guys and choose to focus on him instead.

I find the stage edge, rising up onto my knees. *I'm so close you could touch. Do you want to?* My body tempts and teases as my hands drop to my hips. My nails scrape against my pale flesh, drawing lines of lust while peeling down my thong. I'm not worried about being naked. I never am. It is all part of the game and I am the best player.

I know you are looking at my pussy. It is inviting you in.

I run my hand down seductively between my legs as the stage plunges into darkness.

My arm sweeps through the shadows as I try to collect all the dollar bills I can. I know I will get the remainders, but it's a habit I haven't broken from the good old days, before Venmo and card. The days when we would have to hover around naked,

The Senator's Daughter

picking up every dollar. Now Chuck deals with it all. I trust him more than I do myself when it comes to spending my money.

As I stand, letting the darkness cover me, my gaze seeks out the woman out again. I have seen all sorts of people, from all walks of life, inside this place. I don't judge. I don't care who you are or what brought you through the doors. We all have a story, right?

But she just doesn't fit. It's not about the expensive clothes or her fancy salon-styled hair or the fact that she quite obviously has never stepped foot in a place like this before. It's deeper, a look in her eyes, a part of her that calls out to me, that says *I don't belong here.* It makes me wonder: where does she belong?

4

WILLOW

I slide inside my inner-city apartment, my back against the door as it closes, slipping off the designer heels that were just not made to be worn for that number of hours. I'm lucky. My parking space costs more a year than a lot of people's rent, and although the apartment is mine and in my name, it was absolutely not bought and paid for by me. Instead, it was a gift from my parents for graduating.

I'm Willow Rutherford. The only daughter of Senator Rutherford. I almost never announce my last name because it makes a room go silent when I do, and I've never felt comfortable with it. My brothers have no issues, they dine on it every single chance they get and then some. Maybe the problem is that I'm more like my grandmother, perhaps because of the time I spent studying outside the US. Or maybe it's just a switch in my brain that causes me to shudder at the thought of having to use the name Rutherford to get somewhere in life.

Don't get me wrong. I am grateful. I know my privilege. I'm under no illusions about the opportunities it gives me: my career, my apartment, and even my looks, due to the nose I had straightened at sixteen.

I don't undervalue it, but and I certainly don't see it as a right.

The privilege causes a distance, though, between me and my family. A coldness we have all grown to accept, and this has been made harder because I am the only girl of five. My parents' one hope for a daddy's girl, or the best friend my mom always wanted in a daughter. We tried, repeatedly, but their values were so different from my own. I was consistently disappointed by both of them, so I worked on creating distance between us.

It was a transition. I spent less time at the enormous family estate and more time taking a quick lunch. Accepting a drop-off with a smile. Checking in by phone rather than meeting up for dinner. Time, patience, and politeness have been the real key to cementing the relationship we have now, though there have been times when the boundaries have been crossed.

I drop my keys into the bowl and start to peel off my clothing as I meander my way through my apartment, opening the fridge to disappointment because the health-kick me did the shopping this week. As I sip on cold water and snack on some low-everything bar that certainly isn't giving me the sugar rush I crave, I think about her. The dark haired dancer from the club.

I have experimented with my sexuality, as most girls do at an all-girls boarding school. Being overseas gave me the freedom to explore and the reassurance that my parents were not likely to hear about it on the ivy league social grapevine.

But I had never experienced a reaction like that--not just to a woman, but to anyone.

My brief sexual dalliances with girls began and ended in boarding school. Once I returned to the States, I was hyper-focused on studying and didn't think about dating at all. However, my mother had other ideas and every so often I would cave and date the next preppy "Good future husband and father to my children" that she chose for me, but I had a three-month rule. Anything more than three months and expectations became solid. You were on *a path.*

So as soon as those ninety days were over, I gracefully excused myself from the man's life with the promise that it wasn't him, it was me. (Spoiler: It was him. They were all awful.) I told him I hoped he would find all he was looking for in life. (That was a lie, too, because I couldn't have cared less.)

And that had been my dating life to date. Sex-wise I'm not a nun. I occasionally hook up with guys who are not Rutherford-approved, but who satisfy an ache. Or else a vibrating variety of pleasure I keep tucked away for rainy days. But I have never looked at a woman, not really, the way I had found myself looking at her.

It wasn't just the fact she was the sexiest woman I had ever seen. It was the way she held herself like she didn't care if she was or wasn't sexy to anyone else, only that she felt it. And that, in turn, made me feel it. That made my body ache for her in ways I had only begun to imagine.

I had wanted to step up on that stage and touch

her, taste her, devour her. Not just her body, but her thoughts, her mind, her story.

Is it because the nature of what she does is designed to create desire and arousal? It can't just be that, because I saw a number of dancers that night who held no interest for me.

Just her. She was exquisite, in every way. My body had felt alive with desire when I watched her dance. I hadn't been able to look away for a second as she threw herself around the pole, quickly then slowly, as though she was making love to the pole itself. I wanted her to ride my face in the way her lovely long thighs rode that pole.

Her body was almost impossibly beautiful. She looked too perfect to be real, as though she had been made artificially--although there was nothing to suggest cosmetic surgery. Her breasts were big, full, and round and and they swayed in a way that suggested they were real. Her waist was tiny and then her hips flared out into a beautiful feminine hourglass shape, topped off by her beautiful beautiful ass--as full and round and peachy as any I had ever seen.

Her eyes were this incredible dark blue like none I had ever seen before. She fixed her gaze on me a couple of times as she danced and we had a moment, just a moment where time froze and I thought we had a connection. I thought I could see into her soul for a split second--and then it was gone.

I wanted more.

I want more.

When she rolled her tiny panties down I couldn't draw my gaze away. I felt my mouth watering as I looked at her pussy. I felt bereft as the room went dark and the sight of her body was taken away from me.

As I come back to the present moment and put the water away, I shake my head. I make my way to bed, knowing full well that I will not sleep properly again until I know more about her. I can't get her out of my head.

"Thanks for being a good sport last night, Wills." Simon is leaning over the edge of my booth at a respectable distance, but with a low enough voice to not be overheard. "I know it isn't always the easiest situation we put you in around here . . . but you know, good that you make the effort. It makes a difference. Right or wrong, they respect you more for it. Hope you didn't spend too much." He finishes with a smile and I return it softly.

"No problem. The reports you wanted are on your desk, and I also finished the project analysis Jeff was asking about the other day. I know you don't need it right now, but I thought it might help with the meeting tomorrow if you had the outline for the diversification plans."

Simon's eyebrows raise slightly and I see the wheels in motion as he begins to nod. "Actually, that could be really helpful in pushing the budget in the right direction." He gives the top of my desk a little tap. "Thanks, Wills. I don't know what we would do without you." He is already gone, half in his office, head in the meeting tomorrow—exactly where it should be and not thinking about my strip club spending.

I go to the gym after work. Not because I want to work out at all, but so I can get rid of some excited energy and soak under the shower after. Then change into something more appropriate for my evening plans.

Generally, I imagine women in strip clubs want to stand out and be noticed. Be seen. I do not. So I go for dark pants, a black shirt, my hair up, and subtle sweeps of makeup. I take the same spot at the bar as the previous night and the waitress gives me a warm smile before sliding me the same drink from the night before. I see all too clearly how this could begin a habit.

It fills a desire so effortlessly. Except . . . I'm not one of the desperate men in here. I know what I want and I know how to get it. Well, mostly.

"How do I get a dance? Private?" I ask, sounding confident.

The waitress doesn't even blink, simply leans forward. "With a specific girl?"

I nod, and I know she knows which one without me saying a word. I must have been more obvious than I thought. Her head nods to the side. "Take your drink to the second booth. Get comfortable, pay the amount on the account in there. Private dance is all yours."

I take my drink, standing slowly but walking with the confidence I don't really feel. I have written my name and number on a piece of paper and wrapped it around a bundle of cash. Money is easy for me. Getting what I want with it is also easy for me. I'm still a Rutherford; let's not forget.

It will be her choice if she calls later or not. I promise myself I won't come back if she doesn't.

5
LOLA

I get a tap on my dressing room door followed by a note asking for a VIP dance-- Lola specifically. A new client. That's the kind of request we crave, the ones that turn a slow night into a big earner. And I know if I give a new client a good time, they will become a Lola superfan and give me plenty of repeat business. I glance at the mirror one last time, not that I have any doubt. I know I look sexy as fuck.

I slip inside the booth, its darkness illuminated by a neon purple glow. Soft leather seats form a semicircle with a table and pole in the middle. The steps up are narrow. My skyscraper plexiglass heels mean I have to take the stairs slowly, but they also make the curve of my instep look sexy and show off my perfectly painted purple toes. *Wouldn't you like to start there and work your way up?* they ask, in a way only a good pair of shoes ever could.

I recognize the woman even before I catch her gaze. She sits in her suit, shirt loosened, looking almost casual this time. Drink in hand.

I might have been surprised that it was her, but I'm not. I remember how closely she watched me dance last night. I remember the hunger in her eyes.

It will make a pleasant change to dance privately for a woman. Neither of us speak.

My hands drop to my waist and I pull the knot on my silky robe. The fabric falls straight to the floor in the spectacular way that silk does.

I watch her gaze drag up my body as I stand tall in the center of the table. Her eyes are hazel, I think. Brownish gold with flecks of amber. Beautiful.

Watch me.

The pole behind me rests between my shoulder blades and my hips thrust forward, so she has no choice but to let her eyes linger over my curves--drinking in every dollar she is paying for.

The woman looks composed and immaculate one minute and nervous and flighty the next. She reminds me of a beautiful gazelle as her golden eyes flicker and scan my body. She licks her lips; she is hungry for me.

I've done this so many times before. I start into my well-rehearsed routine.

I slide down the pole. My knees spread wide, thighs parting, and my tiny black thong barely hides my sex. My head falls back, hair cascading down my back, and this thrusts my chest forward. The neon light glides over my skin, lighting me up, and my breasts spill from the silky fabric of my bra.

My hands reach up and take the pole, my body rising before I spin. I dance for myself as much as I dance for her. I love to dance and to feel eyes on my body. I let the rhythm pulse through my veins, every thought in my head laced with sex. My leg curls around the cold, thick steel and I gasp as I feel that cool press against my pussy through the silk. I feel myself getting wet and I like it.

My knees find the floor. The steel is polished to perfection, so my inner thighs reflect off the surface as I crawl forward. My eyes meet hers, wide and full of that good girl need to please--but with edges of steel that tell this woman that I could have her on her knees in seconds, worshipping me, if I wanted.

My palms rest against my stomach, sliding upwards and cupping my breasts, lifting their weight before I let them go with a bounce. My fingers continue higher, teasing over my chest to my neck where I pull the string. And finally, my breasts are free and her gaze is on them. I wonder if she realizes that she is leaning forward.

We move in sync as my legs swing from the table. She finishes her drink and sets it aside. My heels find the floor and I turn, so close to being naked except for that tiny slither of black silk that slips between my cheeks. As I bend forward, I feel her hand on my ass. Clients aren't supposed to touch us. I know she will have read this when she signed up to this, but sometimes I let touching slide and this time is one such occasion.

Her hand feels good on my ass.

I arch my back and push back into her touch and feel her grab a handful of my flesh. Electricity runs through me. My job is sexually charged in general, and at times like this, extremely so.

I spin on one heel, knees rising up onto the leather to straddle her lap. I drop my hips and drag my pussy against her pants. She looks as though she might explode at any second. Her hands are instinctively on my thighs. I choose to let them remain there.

Up close, her face is beautiful. I like the sharpness of her cheekbones and the lovely heart shape of her face. I like her expensive looking hair that is a million shades of honeyed gold glinting in the lights.

She is clearly from a very different world than the one I inhabit, and it seems wild that our paths have collided here. Resulting in my straddling and grinding down on her.

I usually do the grinding for effect only, but right now I'm doing it for my own pleasure. I feel pressure against my clitoris and I like it. I moan involuntarily and watch her eyes widen. Her pupils dilate. She gulps, anxiously.

I know I am very wet and I wonder if she is too.

I wonder if she will think of me later. If she will ache for me. If she will dream about how good I would be to touch, to taste.

My body tells her how good sex with me would be. I would blow her fucking mind.

My hands reach up to the ceiling, stretching my body out, and I rise up higher, moving my pussy away from her lap. I look down, watching my breasts trail upwards against her. I lower my hands to run my fingers through her perfectly blowdried golden hair, guiding her soft chin to the perfect angle so I can feed her desires.

I offer my breast to her lips and I know I am going to let her take it.

My nipple hovers barely a centimetre from her pale pink painted lips.

A couple of seconds pass almost as though she is giving herself permission before she opens her mouth. I sigh, letting her reach out her tongue to glaze my nipple. I lean forward so she can feel the weight of my breasts against her pretty face, drowning her in my femininity. Then I rise higher. Her open mouth tries to take more. I feel the drag of her teeth down my stomach. She is inching closer and closer to my pussy and I can feel her gasps against my skin.

As I stand over her, I lift my right leg and rest my heel on a ledge. My legs are wide open for her now. I reach for her shirt, pulling her to me as I thrust my hips forward. The silky cotton of my thong is the only barrier between my sex and her eager tongue, and I feel her mouth grazing against it, desperate to take a bite. The heat of her breath warms my clit.

I look down into her amber eyes as she looks up at me. She is flushed, needy, eager, and wanting. And so am I. I want her to take that taste and yet—I pull her back. Our allotted time is just about finished anyway, but that is not the true cause of my abruptness. She reaches up and her fingers run down my stomach, hooking in the band of my panties. A wad of bills is tucked inside.

I feel a disappointment that I never have before. This was a transaction--an exchange taking place at the same time that my mind and body had drifted. I had started to believe it was something else. I flash her the famous Lola smile, step out of her space, and slip away, shaking away the feelings as I walk.

What was I thinking, anyway? I have no idea who that woman is, but she is here for one thing and one thing only—just like every other girl and guy who have come through the door before and everyone who will come after.

I sit down heavily in front of the mirror as I wipe away the makeup. I'm done for the night. I have time for another dance, but I no longer have the will nor the motivation in me. Plus, I made plenty on that last one. I slip the bundle of money from my panties and slam it down harder than I intended on the dresser. *Maybe I really am getting too old for all this shit*, I think with a sigh.

Then I notice it. The note wrapped up under the band. I peel it out slowly, my fingers unfolding the soft pink edges, because of course a girl like her would have pastel notes to pass to strippers in wads of cash.

A name and a number. Did it need more? No, it's enough to shake the mood I have been in and a glow runs through me. It wasn't a payment, she had slipped me a note in the only way she knew how to via the private dance and the tip, and as the pad of my fingertip runs over the piece of paper, I feel the softness of her name fall from my lips. "Willow."

What should I do with my day off? Spend it overthinking about a phone number? You are absolutely correct. I unfolded and folded the paper so much that if I hadn't already memorized it, I might not have been able to make the numbers out.

My mind has been going a million miles an

hour trying to come up with all the reasons it's a bad idea to text her. To try and help, I started a list:

1. You barely know anything about her.

2. She is definitely very rich.

3. I bet it is some kink, uptown girl thing going on.

4. Terrible idea to date a client.

5. I don't even know what she wants.

6. I could lose a lot of tips if I start giving out free dances at home...

That one I added to make myself smile, which it did. And of course I had counter answers for them all with a list of reasons why I should text her. And what it all boiled down to was this: What did I want and what did I have to lose?

So, here I am now, taking out my phone, adding her name and number, and typing quickly. I press send without a pause.

Hey Willow. It's Lola from McLandons. How are you?

I want to curl up into my sofa and die. Except it smells like something already has, so I decide now would be a really good time to not stare at my phone and actually clean up. My apartment is slightly bigger than a studio. And I wish I could say that I kept it in tip-top shape, but I can be messy. Not dirty, but there are things. Everywhere.

The problem with working nights and feeling like a vampire during the day is that you kind of lose your motivation to pick shit up when you could just turn off a light, *and taa-daa*, the mess is gone. But everything does have a place and it's just laziness that stops me from doing it, so I push myself to turn my phone over and work through the mess that has spread.

A quick dash turns into a two-hour upend, moving things around and making a list of new things I want to buy that I probably don't need. I finally collapse on my freshly vacuumed sofa and slowly turn my phone over, feeling the butterflies as I look down to see that little notification box glowing.

Lola . . . I don't know what I expected, but it suits you. Feeling much better now. Would you like to get a drink sometime? Willow.

I feel my cheeks turn pink, Lola does suit me—it's why I chose it, but I like that she thinks so as well. I reply.

A drink sounds good. Let me know when and where.

Tonight, 8pm, Suitopia. I notice she doesn't hesitate to respond.

I will see you there.

6

WILLOW

She made me wait all day. I mean, she might have been sleeping--I don't know the exact schedule of sleep when it comes to her profession. But I still checked my phone every few minutes. Made myself get up and make a coffee while I left the phone behind on the desk, trying to pretend it wasn't the first thing that I wanted to check the moment I sat down.

When her first message came, it was her name that made me smile the most. Lola. I have never met anyone called Lola before, and of all the names in the world I could have imagined, Lola wasn't one I would have thought of. And yet, the moment I saw it in the text, I could see that was who she was. Inside and out. Lola.

I'm not down for playing games. In the just few minutes we shared together, I saw more of her body than I have ever seen of my own. I felt her flesh on mine, smelled her sex, tasted her skin. I don't need to play phone tennis for a week in order to make plans. I want to know more than her body.

Suitopia is a good option for our meeting. Middle of the city, neutral ground, not so fancy that I would run into anyone who has my mother on speed dial, but also not divey. Just a nice cocktail bar where the drinks taste good and the music fills the silence, but you can still lean in, talk, and get to know someone.

I made a lot of effort, then spent the rest of the time in front of the mirror making it look like I hadn't. Ruffled up ponytail, slightly smudged makeup after a perfect application. My shirt had been tucked and untucked so many times that I surrendered and tucked it in the end to hide the creases I had made.

Lola is already there when I arrive, not at the bar but at a table. I smile because it is exactly the one I would have chosen. I wonder if my desire for her will be as strong as it was on that night, now that her clothes are on. She still doesn't see me, so I take a moment to check her out.

Her hair is down in long messy dark curls, which makes her look like she has just stepped out of a shampoo ad. And she's facing me, perched on a high stool. Although she is slightly hidden from my view, I can see she's wearing jeans and a tight tee shirt. Nothing fancy. She is effortlessly gorgeous. So many women would spend hours in front of a mirror and still never look as good as that. Lola is natural, beautiful. My smile turns into a grin as I approach.

"Hey," she says, her voice trailing off. She smiles back. I realize this is the first time hearing her voice. It's sweet like honey, and soft. If Lola had called me on the phone, I would have thought she was much younger, yet that sweetness suits her. She has an innocence you would never see on stage.

"Hey to you too," I reply, as I step up and sit on a chair, slowly unwrapping my scarf as I reach for a cocktail menu. "What did you order?" I ask, with a nod to her glass.

"A Showgirl," Lola says with a grin. I laugh.

"The perfect choice. Will you choose mine?" I slide the menu across and her eyes widen.

"What? So much pressure! I don't know what you like. I could make a horrible choice and then you would most definitely judge me."

I laugh at her genuine concern. "I won't judge you. Surprise me. I like surprises."

Lola's eyebrows lift questioningly. "Well, that surprises me. You don't seem like the type to enjoy surprises at all. In fact, I already had you figured for a 'life plan at eighteen' kind of woman."

"Try fifteen," I say, with a wry smile. "But that's just one side of my life. The other . . . I like to feel the surprise in other areas." My voice trails off as a server arrives. Lola points to the menu, ordering me something. I don't care what it is. I know I will like it just because she chose it.

Small talk has never been my best skill. I find it awkward and a complete waste of time. But Lola is a chatterbox. Words tumble from her lips in a neverending flow of warmth and genuine curiosity, which makes me find everything she has to say interesting.

As her green eyes glitter with excitement, and I find myself swept away by her childlike joy.

The waiter brings over my drink. I can see right away that I would never have chosen it. An exuberant display of excess—cream and chocolatey swirls with who knows what blend of alcohol.

But I smile at Lola over the top of my glass, leaning in as my lips part and my tongue extends to find the straw. I take it in and give a slow suck, feeling the cold blend of ice cream, alcohol and other flavors I can't put my finger on.

The drink is delicious. Like a dessert made for adults, creamy with a kick of naughtiness. I take a longer sip than I planned because it just tastes that good. I watch Lola settle back in her seat with an almost smug smile on her face.

"You like?" she asks playfully, and I nod with a smile.

"I really do."

I watch Lola move almost in slow motion when, as the straw slips from my lips, she sits forward, reaching. The pad of her thumb runs across my bottom lip. I feel the cream smear as she does it, then I see it on her thumb as she pulls away. Without even a second thought, she slips it between her own lips and sucks it clean.

It is the single sexiest thing I have ever seen and it nearly makes me gasp out loud.

"Maybe a little too creamy for me, but I had you down as the secret sweet tooth type," she says with a smile. Lola seems almost oblivious to the effect she has on me.

"Maybe a little, but keep it to yourself," I remind her.

"I want to know more of your secrets," Lola says. Her lack of filter, her directness--it's refreshing. She catches me off guard and makes me feel tingles at the same time.

"You can ask me anything," I say, as I take another drink of my creamy delight.

"Hamburger or hotdog?"

"Burger."

"Yellow or blue?"

"Blue."

"Born rich or self-made?"

"Born." Not even a flicker at the answer, so I know she already knew.

"Lesbian, bi, or just curious?"

I screw my face up at the question.

If only I knew.

"No idea," I say. That brings a flicker of contemplation to her eyes, but it's barely there before it's gone.

"You?" I put the same question back to her before she has chance to ask something else, and Lola rewards me with a smile.

"I didn't say you could ask me anything, but in this case I can answer . . . hot dog, yellow, neither, and a lesbian." With that, she finishes her drink. "One more question, then. My place or yours?"

I think about this one. Obviously there is a third answer, but it's not one I'm willing to think about. I want her. I don't care where it happens-- but at the same time, I like to feel in control. I reply, "My place."

We could have walked. I would have walked except it all felt too far, too cold. Too much. So we take a cab, which took only a few minutes, but I am pleased with the choice as we sit in nervous, yet excited silence.

I can't stop thinking of when her pussy was so close to my mouth I could almost taste her, I admit to myself.

I pay and we exit and enter my building. As we walk through the marbled foyer, Lola lets out a low whistle.

"I am pleased you chose your place," she remarks. "I would have died of embarrassment after seeing this."

The elevator dings. We step inside and I give her a tender smile. "I wouldn't be looking at your place as much as I would be looking at you," I say.

Lola turns to me slowly. Even though we are nearly the same height, her eyes are slightly lower than mine, so she has to look up to meet my gaze. I like the way that feels. It makes me feel protective of her, even though she's the one who stops to softly sweep the hair from my cheek. It's a sweet moment. All too quickly, the doors ping open.

"Saved by the bell!" she says, and I laugh as I lead us to my apartment. I fumble with the keys, showing my nerves, but then the door finally swings open.

I really didn't expect to have Lola over tonight, but luckily, I always have wine and a pristine place, so that isn't an issue. Turns out, I don't have to show her around either. Lola is exploring, going in and out of each room, looking at things. She is even opening drawers.

I feel my eyebrows raising. I've never met anyone quite like Lola. There is something so refreshing about her.

I head to the kitchen. "White or red?" I call out.

"White." I hear another cupboard open and close.

"You know, I don't think you're supposed to go through people's houses while they're still there. You're supposed to wait until they've left," I say with a grin. I slide Lola's glass across the counter as she walks through to the kitchen. She shrugs.

"I think it is better to not hide these things. I am interested in you. I have looked and that has piqued my interest more. I've seen the things you choose to show and some of the things you want to hide. It only makes me want to know you more." Lola takes a long, deep drink. I'm surprised she can even taste the wine; she swallowed it so quickly.

Lola leaves the glass on the counter and saunters to the living room. As she settles on my sofa, she looks like she belongs there, her dark hair stark against my creamy suede sofa. Lola is so incredibly beautiful, almost classically so, with her make up more refined than it was while she was working.

"Why don't you come and join me?" she askes softly. As I move toward her, she adds, "Leave the wine."

I do, of course I do. And then I cover the distance as she pats her lap. I feel dizzy, my pulse racing as I slowly straddle her.

"I can feel my heart beating in my chest," I admit as I sit on her lap, my legs softly and slowly spreading, so I can settle on her thighs.

"I wonder where else I can hear it," she says with a low voice. Heat sizzles through the air between us.

"Where do you think?" I ask, but I am nervous, cautious.

"I don't know. Where do you think?" She won't give me an out. Lola wants to push me.

"I imagine you might hear it anywhere if you got close enough. I can feel my heartbeat all through my body."

"Then I'll have to listen all over," she says softly, her voice low as I watch her lips.

"You will."

"I will have to start at your chest," she decides, and I nod.

"I think that's the best place to start," I agree.

Lola leans in slowly, pressing her ear against my chest. My heart is beating loud . . . fast . . . hammering . . . so I try to control it with deep slow breaths. Calm thoughts. But it doesn't work. Still those fast, loud beats, just for her. And Lola listens to every one.

"Don't break it," I whisper softly, wondering

where the words came from. I barely even know her, but this is how I feel, like she has me in the palm of her hand. Right before my hands drop to her jaw, soft palms against her skin, tilting her up. I lean down and give her a kiss on her beautiful, full lips. Lola's lips are so very seductive and kissing them is exactly the thrill I thought it might be. The kiss is deep, slow and delicate, and she kisses me back. Slow. Delicate in return. Letting me know her intention isn't to break my heart.

My lips part a little, just to take a breath of her. Gentle and tentative, I draw her air in. My eyes close and I savor it, savor her. And when my eyes open slowly, I feel the tingles, tiny trembles, so close, so near, that my heartbeat doesn't stand a chance. "It's late," I manage, but even those two words are difficult for me to get out.

She nods and nuzzles against me, placing a kiss right on my chest. "It is," she agrees, but makes no movement away. My fingers are still on her jaw as her head drops to my chest. I thrust my hands back into her wonderful glossy dark hair. The slow run of my fingers through her hair, then a press of my palm, holding Lola right against my chest. "Maybe . . . maybe we should sleep. Rest. You can stay here."

I want to do so much more with her but I feel my inexperience deeply. It is all so overwhelming that I'm not sure where to start.

"Do you think we should sleep?" she asks, and her voice is seductive.

I pause between what I should say and the truth. "Yes," I pause, "but I don't want to," I add.

"Then don't."

"What do you want?" I can hear the edge of neediness in my voice as I ask her.

"You to stay awake with me."

"If I stay awake with you, what will we do?"

"I could make you feel more trembles. More tingles," Lola says softly, and I have no doubt that she could.

"You could . . . but will you?"

She gives me another kiss on my chest and drags her chin along it as she looks back at me. "Yes."

I feel it, instantly, straight between my thighs. The race of my pulse there, the flush of heat. "I want to feel it all."

"What do you want to feel?" she asks and places another kiss on my chest. I can't take my eyes off her. My heart is beating so fast that I feel dizzy with it. Blurring what I think and what I should say. So it all tumbles from me. "I want to feel you."

She kisses down my body so slowly. Lips touching me over and over again. Her tongue drags a little down my body.

I swallow. My mouth feels dry and it's just so hard to catch my breath. So many kisses . . . the drag of her tongue . . . my fingers stretch, then grab the blanket hanging over the sofa, bunching it in my palm. I grip it as I start to tremble harder. And her expert hands move effortlessly over my body, over my clothes, and they start to undo and remove them. But it is all so skillful, so gentle, that I barely notice as I come undone.

She kisses through my trembles as she makes her way down further. She runs along my thigh with her mouth.Down slowly and then back up just as slow, and the slowness is overwhelming . . . I'm aching. Aching for more. My panties stick to me. I'm already so wet. I can feel it, and I feel shy for her to know how little control I have over how much I want her.

She stops and then presses a kiss right against my wet panties and then nuzzles her face in. My clitoris throbs in response.

"Lola . . . Please . . ." I don't know what I'm

saying, what I'm asking. Just that I am desperate for more of her, that I want to feel her tongue against me.

She gives me another kiss and then another. I know she can feel my wetness through my panties. "Please what, baby?" she asks soft and low right against my panties.

Her kisses give me a little pressure, the tease of relief, but it's not enough. Her words vibrate against me. Making me tense and tremble more. "Please . . . please lick me . . . I want to feel your tongue . . ."

"Can you lift up your ass for me, baby?" Her voice is rich like silk.

I nod. My knees press into the sofa, hips slowly thrusting up, holding them there as my ass slowly leaves her lap and she lifts me slowly, lowering me back onto the rug. She slides me into place where she wants me before she moves to the top of my panties and grips them between her teeth. Then she slowly pulls them down, gently moving them down my legs. Her mouth, her nose, runs over my pussy.

"Oh . . ." I let out a moan. I can feel the exposure of the silk of my panties peeling from me, sticking in places because I'm so wet. Then her face runs over me, against me, and it feels so fucking good.

She returns to my pussy and gives me a kiss. A slow one. And then a lick. A deep one.

And I react on instinct. My thighs part further as my eyes close. She kisses my vulva so slowly it's like she is making out with me, then a lick, deep and long, pushing inside me, pulling out of me . . .

She is making me lose my senses.

She is driving me crazy.

Her nose drags along against me. Her tongue flicks and swirls over and over against me.

I can see the mess of her hair between my legs. Her eyes are closed. She looks so incredibly beautiful.

I've never felt like this before during sex. This is something entirely new and completely incredible. I want to give every part of myself to her and take every part of her from her.

My hands reach for her. My nails lightly run up her back to show my hunger and my palm gently rests against the back of her head to show her my need. I draw her face tighter against me as my hips slowly thrust up. I hold her in place, so close to me so all she can breathe and taste and smell is me.

I don't want to take over, but I can't seem to

stop myself. Another run of my nails up her back. My feet slide up, knees bending and spreading outwards so I can open myself completely for her. Then I pull her face against me again. Both hands. And I grind hard. She lets out a moan right into my pussy as I grind against her face. She licks me again and again. Her tongue flicks and swirls as I grind harder, making her struggle to breathe every now and then. When she does, it's all me.

I can feel my own neediness in her, too, in every lick and press against me. She attacks me hungrily with her mouth.

I am needy for her. I need to see my pleasure dripping from her face, no limits or lines. "Does it make you feel like I own you?" I gasp.

"Yes." She nods and I feel her mouth move against me as she does. "It does. It makes me feel like you own me."

"Is that what you want?" My voice is so slow, soft, higher than normal because she is still edging me, bringing me to that place where only she exists in my entire world. "You want to serve me?"

"Yes." She nods again against me. "I want to serve you."

"No lines? No limits?" My fingers tighten in her hair, and I thrust up harder, a deeper grind. Taking her air five . . . ten . . . fifteen . . . twenty seconds. I wonder how long she could drown in my pussy for.

"No lines or limits," she says, struggling to get the words out as I thrust up and grind deeper and take more air away from her.

"I want to cross every line . . . push every limit." She doesn't need words; this is what she needs. I grind again and this time my legs close, curling around her to draw me into her hard, holding her in place. I love that she wants to serve me. Whenever I need to be pleasured, she'll be there, eager for me . . . My thoughts have run wild and so has my body. I tense and wrap tightly around her, feeling it all take over, every single wave of pleasure I take and fall into. I am shaking, trembling, reaching the peak . . . and then I let go. A hot rush of me covers her tongue and her lips, smeared across her face as I orgasm hard with no inhibitions or reservations.

I feel like I black out for a minute. It is hard to tell where I am or what is real. But as the room comes into focus, all I can see is Lola. Covering my skin in kisses. I am naked while she is completely dressed, and the irony isn't lost on me. As if she can hear my thoughts, she looks up at me with a grin.

"I thought it was only fair." And before she can even let out a laugh, I am reaching for her, pulling her to me and on top of me so my lips press hard against hers. I taste me, and her, the perfect blend--a delicious combination that I won't be able to ever get enough of. She collapses onto me and we both give into it, drifting, kissing, and touching each other until the night takes us and we fall asleep, tangled in blankets on the floor.

7
LOLA

There are moments in your life that are so important that a "before" and an "after" are created, with reference to them.

Willow Rutherford came crashing into my life. Despite our very obvious differences, from the moment I felt her on my skin, I knew she was only supposed to taste me more. I left for our date nervous, but the second I saw Willow, I knew she was special and that I wanted her—and I am not the kind of woman to let opportunities slip me by. She was unsure, a confident woman out of her comfort zone. So I took the lead, flirted harder than I perhaps might normally, and pushed myself into her space to show her that what she wanted and what I wanted were the same. Because I knew she wanted me.

It is my job, after all, to read not the things that people say, which are often cloaked by darkness and music. And many words are left unspoken. Instead, I read their bodies, their actions, and the invitations they give away with their eyes without even knowing they are doing it. And Willow's body was like a megaphone, hollering out exactly what she wanted. Her eyes showed nothing but hunger for me. And once she started to let go of her reservations, the words fell from her beautiful lips as well.

She surprised me sexually. And I don't surprise easily.

Her words during our sex were so fucking hot. Willow didn't yet realize that she wanted to really take control--to make me need her, want her, drown in her. And that is exactly what I wanted too.

Willow tasted like heaven to me. I'd have happily drowned in her.

Sleeping on her floor left me achy despite the luxurious floor coverings, however, and the sun was streaming in early, which I wasn't mentally prepared for. I only see one "six o'clock" in a usual day, and it's never the first one. But Willow's body is stunning in the sunlight. Her pale skin is luminous in the morning light and her hair is all kinds of honeyed highlights in easy waves. Maybe a little messy, but not much. Even a post-sex Willow Rutherford who spent the night on the floor is very well put together.

Willow, it seems is an early riser, and the moment her lovely brownish gold eyes open they have a focus I'm envious of.

"Well, good morning, sleepy girl," she says with a warm smile that makes my morning grumpiness fade in seconds. Her teeth are perfect. Not hollywood dazzling white, but a lovely natural shade of white with very neat alignment. I imagine that has something to do with an expensive cosmetic dentist. She is so very pretty.

"Is it morning? . . . I've never seen this mythical thing," I say with a wry smile, as Willow laughs.

"I usually get up at six, but then I get to the office early, or work out--or you know, do things. I think maybe for this one morning, I could do fewer things." I listen to Willow's words, but am aware that her body is telling me more. Her hand reaches to touch me. Her nails are neatly manicured and french polished. Her hand is soft and her touch is gentle and intimate.

"I like fewer things," I reply, but I can hear the little shift in my own voice. It's almost thickening with want.

What is it about Willow Rutherford that is so enticing to me?

In my line of work, it would be easy to make assumptions that I often sleep with clients. Either for money or otherwise. I know that some of the girls do, but for me it couldn't be further from the truth. Maybe it helps that most of my clients are men and I'm just not interested in men. I never have been.

Willow is the first. My first time meeting a client outside of the club. My first time sleeping with a client.

For all the sexual charge I have at work, most of my actual sex is solo. Had alone, at home.

Willow leans in slowly to kiss me, as though it is the most natural move in the world. As though we have kissed a million times before.

Her lips press against mine like I am made of glass. She is so sweet and delicate this morning.

So I give her a really delicate kiss back, super

slow, soft, gentle and shy--but I make sure she can feel me linger before I pull away.

I want her to know that I like it.

God knows what this is between us, or where this is going. I'm no expert in one-night stands, but I'm sure that waking up and tenderly kissing the morning after sex isn't the norm for a casual hook up.

Willow gives me a soft squeeze. I lean forward, resting against her, nuzzling into her. I feel desperate to be close to her and I know how much she craves me like this. "You can lean right here, baby. Okay?" she says, as she gives me another kiss back.

I nod seriously. Sitting exactly where Willow indicates, closing my eyes as she kisses me back, and letting my need wash over me. I feel safe in her arms. Very safe.

"Feels good, doesn't it?" she murmurs softly.

I nod again. I'm not sure I'll be able to find words right now.

"It's okay. Needy girls don't need to talk, do they? And you are a very pretty, needy girl." Willow is confident when she is with me. I never thought of myself as needy and submissive, yearning for a strong capable mommy type, yet here I am. And I like it.

Who is she?

I look up at her under my lashes, trying to find my thoughts, but they're all jumbled up. I shake my head and don't try to talk. I feel myself blush, my eyes lowering shyly as Willow says I'm pretty.

She strokes my cheek delicately with long, graceful fingers. "Oh, I think you might be a special one. So rare. So pretty. So special." I look up into her eyes and I see the shift, the change within her, as she embraces this side of her. Effortlessly, I'm in the headspace where she needs me to be. A headspace I've never been in before. I feel so delicate and I shiver under every gentle touch, as though I might break. It feels like Willow could break me in a second, yet I am still so drawn to her. As her fingers stroke my cheek, I turn my head into her hand and give a tiny kiss, right against her palm.

Almost as if Willow can read my mind, as she tells me, "I could, but I won't. I'll never hurt you, I promise. I just want to make you feel good with my touch. It's okay. I won't shatter you. You're far too beautiful to shatter."

A little noise escapes my lips. I don't recognize

this sound ... a cross between a whimper and a moan. I do feel good. So good. My lips kiss up her palm to her wrist, my tongue sweeping over her skin, feeling her pulse as I take a little taste of her.

"Taste good, baby?"

I nod fast. "You taste so good."

"You're so lucky. You can taste as much of me as you want."

I am so lucky. I feel it, feel like it's making me glow. I keep kissing up her arm. Sometimes just kisses ... other times licks ... and then light warm sucks.

All the time she is stroking me with soft, light touches.

I am barely wearing anything—only what she gave me to sleep in. A silky top with thin straps. Little shorts that match. All for bed ... to feel safe and soft. But I want her touches under them. I edge the straps off my shoulders, shrugging them away and the camisole drops to my hips. I'm naked now from my hips up.

"Oh, such a needy baby." Her hands stroke softly on my shoulders and then she strokes down over my breast.

I am needy. So needy. Every touch of hers makes me tremble. The stroke over my breast is so intense. Her fingers glide, following the curve of my breast. I can't help it; I moan for her.

Willow's hands go lower, inching their way toward the little shorts. Slowly, she works her hand under them. I am hyper-aware of everything. I can feel my own heart beating wildly. My panties are so wet, embarrassingly so, and I'm ashamed for her to know, so I try to close my thighs. But it's too late. Her fingers are under my panties, pushing my legs apart. Willow touches my wetness and I melt into her touch.

My pussy is hidden away, but I feel so exposed. I have nowhere to hide as I sit exactly where she told me to. Against her, leaning into her. Her fingers begin to touch me, exploring my sex so slowly and gently with the same soft light touches that she has been using all along, and I completely lose my mind for her.

This is sex in a way I've never known it. It is sex in a way I've never known I've needed.

She continues to stroke me so nicely. "You do such a good job sitting still. So I will have to give you all those touches you crave so much," she whispers softly to me, her voice so sweet and calming that I feel my whole body shiver in response.

My nipples are swollen and erect.

Fuck, I don't think I've ever wanted anything more than to be her baby. I lean in, trying to hold in my moans as I give her the most delicate of kisses. I listen to her wet fingers stroking back and forth through my folds until they slowly slide inside of me. One finger and then two. She kisses me back and I think I might explode.

I need her so much. I need her more than anything else. Her fingers moving deep inside me make me feel full and as though I belong to her.

I moan into the kiss. I'm so close. So very close.

What the hell is happening to me? I'm usually strong and independent. I'm usually the one leading the sex. Yet here I am, completely vulnerable and coming apart at the touch of her fingers.

I could walk away and protect myself. The thought has crossed my mind more than once. *But why would I ever want to when I'm only whole when you're with me, inside me?* Then the thoughts crash around in my head and consume me.

My whole body craves Willow. I know she can feel it, see it, and hear it as I start to push my hips toward her.

I want more.

I feel her add a third and fourth finger and curl

them inside working them into me, seeking my G spot.

My lips rest against hers, parted. I'm no longer kissing, just giving her every single whimper, moan, gasp, and beg.

"Please...uh...Willow..."

"You feel so good..."

"I need you..."

"More...please...fill me..."

Her fingers work me so good as I find myself folding back into her arm. She is holding me relaxed in her left arm as her right hand works my body like a puppet.

She begins to fuck me now, finding the perfect rhythm effortlessly.

Willow seems to know exactly when to slow down, to draw me out, and when to quicken, to feed my ache. I'm shaking so hard, tightening around her fingers. I'm losing any control I've ever had.

I feel myself squirt around her fingers. Once. Twice. Three times.

I lose count.

Suddenly I feel more pushing inside of me. It is the rest of her hand.

It hurts for just a second as my body stretches

open for her. Then her knuckles slide inside me and it feels suddenly very easy. I've just taken her whole hand inside me--and it feels easy.

I reach down and realize I can feel her wrist. Her whole hand is in me. She starts to move it slowly but surely, back and forth. I feel her knuckles against my G spot.

Oh, fuck. Fuck. Fuck.

"Open your eyes and look at me," she says and my eyes flicker open obediently.

Her eyes are flooded with the hunger she has for me and her pupils are wide with lust. She doesn't take her gaze away from mine and I daren't move mine from hers. We are locked together. In that moment, I never want us to be apart.

"I want to come for you," I moan. I'm pleading.

"You can come for me, baby. Come with my whole hand inside you."

"I want to belong to you," I hear myself gasp between hurried breaths. I'm so close, but I've never come before without anything on my clitoris.

"You do. You are all mine," Willow growls, fixing me with the intensity of her gaze. I know she means it.

And I explode.

My orgasm crashes through my body from the depths of my pussy to the tips of my fingers and toes. I feel it everywhere. I come, and I come, and I come some more.

I feel tears in my eyes. I'm crying as I feel my whole body curl up, still held by her, still with her hand deep inside me.

My mind is lost to her, making six a.m. my new favorite time of day.

I am an independent woman. I am very aware of my body and I exert control over it. I also use it to control others. I have done so for most of my adult life. And I have had great, amazing sex before. It's not like I was finally discovering how good it could be.

But sex with Willow Rutherford isn't within the normal realm of sex, either. Nor is it a BDSM power play of dominance. I don't want or need to be physically restrained. The control Willow has over me is mental. It is in the way she edges my body. It is in the way she gives and pauses, teases and toys with me while filthy words drip from her lips like honey. I am a butterfly, addicted to her sweet, sweet nectar.

She is mommy-like in her sweet, gentle brand of dominance and care for me.

This has flipped a switch in me. It has helped my usually full head to feel empty and clear. I have a new lightness about me.

Willow would never need to tie me down. She could tell me to lie still and I wouldn't move an inch.

Is it just a wild lustful affair? Honestly, right now I can't tell, and I haven't asked.

We both seem cautious of discussing the magic between us---as though by voicing it, we might accidentally burst the bubble of happiness we are in.

Willow and I have spent most of our time together naked in one way or another. And the second that sex isn't in the air, the power dynamic between us shifts. I take control of the conversation, tease, and flirt. I'm confident and much more my usual self and Willow seems to settle into a softness that I'm not sure is her natural state but one still she feels comfortable in. I even saw her blush once or twice.

Many days blended into one. We have both

sacrificed pretty much everything in our lives to spend time together. It is strange how quickly your life can entwine with another person's, and in this case it is almost effortless.

Willow lives such a busy life that it makes me tired just to see her calendar. And I live a life of the night, rarely seeing the sunrise other than on a late walk home.

We live in different worlds, clearly. I haven't asked about her family, but it is apparent that even though her job is well paid, there is another source of funding. Beyond that, there is a casual classiness to Willow that only seems to be there in the truly wealthy. She has an easy attitude toward money and spending, which seems to be the exclusive privilege of someone who has never had to worry about working or affording rent. Come to think of it, I'm pretty sure someone like Willow has never rented anything. People like Willow buy things. Expensive things. Like her luxurious apartment and everything in it.

I've always had to worry about earning money and affording rent.

Don't get me wrong. I do well financially. I make great money from tips and private dances. I am not struggling. But it wasn't always this way.

Money drives me. No-one else will pay for me if I don't.

But despite our differences, we have effortlessly entwined ourselves with one another. One day we were two separate people, then in the way lesbians have done since the dawn of time (I imagine)—ever since that night we first had sex, we melted into one and have barely been apart since.

I sleep while she works, and I wake to messages of lust and longing. I catch Willow after her long days and we eat, laugh, and talk. And then usually we have sex once, twice, three times. However long we can fit in until I have to leave for the club.

Sometimes she'll come to the club and watch me from her spot at the bar, her eyes on me. I can feel them. I dance for Willowe now. When she is there and even when she isn't. I feel her hungry eyes on my body and I just want to please her.

I don't mind taking my clothes off for men and their money. I never have. Luckily, Willow doesn't seem to mind either. It is nothing but transactional and I enjoy that it doesn't cause her insecurity. Willow Rutherford is very secure in every way. She loves watching me dance.

Everything builds until the moment I can have

8

WILLOW

I look in the mirror and see that I'm still the same woman. I still have the same reflection. I still have the same goals, the same wants, and the same needs. But there is a difference. I don't want to be all dramatic and I certainly don't believe in all those romance novels, but I can see it in me. There's no denying it.

I knew that I liked control in my personal life as well as my professional one. But Lola made me see just how deep that ran in me. It was a surprise. I'm happy to see her sparkle and I love watching her flirt. She surprises me with her directness-- how she can say or do something that others may only think about.

Then it all changes in a second and her body sings for me. She comes apart just for me. Sometimes I don't even know what I'm saying: I just seem to know what Lola needs to hear to make her magical navy blue eyes fill with devotion.

I'm obsessed with her. With us, and what we are together.

I watch her dance in the club when I can. I feel the sting of jealousy when I see the men looking at her with lust, but it's only natural and I let myself feel it. But I also revel in the knowledge that for every dollar that gets tucked into Lola's panties, it will be me that she goes home with. And that makes everything ok.

Lola isn't interested in them. She is interested in me, only me. And I don't doubt that for a second.

Lola is an actor, a performer. Lola gives what she needs to give to survive in life.

Her body and face make a living for her. But, at the same time, Lola loves it. She loves the adoration. She loves the effect she has on people when she is nude, smearing neon paint over her incredible God-given body.

And it feels like a privilege to see her do something that she loves, however unconventional.

But it isn't just about the sex with Lola. For a woman in her late twenties, Lola acts like a teenage girl. She lives her life purely for enjoyment and the for sheer joy of being. For someone who doesn't see much of the daylight hours, every moment of the night belongs to her. This city that I know like the back of my hand by day becomes a whole new place in the darkness. I love discovering it with her.

"Let's go to the Big Easy," she says, dragging me out the back of McLandon's, a huge smile on her face.

"Big Easy? Why does that sound like the kind of place I won't like?" I ask. I wrap my arm around Lola anyway and let her lead the way. She laughs.

"Oh, you'll see, your Gucci won't be noticed there, but they make a *mean* JD and coke, and Mac is pretty cool."

The Big Easy was a downtown dive bar. As far as I was concerned, it was a gritty, run-down establishment located right in the city's urban core. We enter. The atmosphere is dark and dingy, with a mix of old bar stools and tables that have seen better days. The walls are adorned with neon beer signs, vintage memorabilia, and graffiti.

The bar serves cheap drinks in large measures-

-in plastic cups--and the music is loud and eclectic, ranging from classic rock to punk to hip hop.

The clientele is a mixed bag of locals, regulars, and tourists alike, all looking for a cheap drink and a good time, and my gaze drifts over them as we make our way through. The conversations are lively, with groups of people sharing stories, jokes, and local gossip.

As I settle on a stool, I can see why Lola likes it here. Mac, the bartender, is friendly and down-to-earth, providing a sense of warmth and familiarity that is often lacking in the more upscale establishments I typically find myself in.

And to my surprise, I like it. A downtown dive bar may not be the most glamorous or trendy spot in town, but the Big Easy has its own unique charm and character.

"See," she says with a playful wink, as she nudges my knee with her hand. Then, to the bartender, "We will take two of your finest and best, Mac!"

He gives her a smile and I can see the twinkle in his eye. I wonder how many guys she has had that effect on. The Lola Effect is still very much present, even when she is fully and casually dressed in jeans and a t-shirt. Her body still sings from beneath her clothes, her incredible skin is still shiny and bronze, and her eyes are still that other worldly dark blue. Most of all, there is her dazzling smile and childlike charm.

Lola's joy and beauty is infectious and I'm not the only one who feels it. I notice this everywhere we go together.

People fall in love with Lola a little bit every day. She easily charms everyone she meets. It doesn't make me question myself. I know who I am. I am confident in my sense of self. Still, it makes me wonder if I would be happier if I weren't always so distant from people.

I watch Mac make the drinks, generous pourings, the right amount of ice and a splash of soda stream coke that looks thick and sugary. He slides the glasses across the bar to us, with a straw for good measure.

I think college was the last time I drank out of a plastic cup with a straw. While I feel the nostalgia, I also feel that Mac does indeed make a killer JD and coke, and I'm suitably impressed.

"I swear it's the straw," Lola says with a smile. I can't help but laugh.

"Maybe it's the company," I say softly, and

watch the way she plays with the straw with her tongue.

Then she looks up at me with a nervous smile. "Well... speaking of company..."

The timing couldn't have been more perfect. The second she starts to speak, the door swings open. It takes me a few seconds to see why this dive bar might be more popular than others and why Mac might be a little friendlier than most.

The dancers of McLandon's, Lola's work friends, descend on the scene in a haze of perfumed air, giggles, cigarette smoke and an aura of sex that can almost be seen pulsing in the air. They are wrapped up and dressed for a change, but I can still see the glisten of oil on the flashes of bare skin. They shrug off their coats.

Lola's girlfriends saunter through, their laughter echoing through the dimly lit space. Dressed to the nines in shimmering, revealing outfits, they are the center of attention as all eyes turn toward them. Their high-heeled shoes click against the scuffed wooden floors as they make their way to the bar.

Despite the stares of the regular patrons, the girls seem to be enjoying themselves, their laughter and playful banter filling the room. They order drinks with a wink and a smile, eliciting chuckles and flattery from Mac.

As they gather around a table in the corner, their conversation grows louder and more animated, occasionally punctuated with bursts of raucous laughter. They seem to be oblivious to the stares and whispers of the other patrons--enjoying each other's company and the carefree atmosphere of the dive bar. Their presence lends an air of glamour and mystique to an otherwise sleepy place, and for a moment, the dive bar feels like the most exciting place in the world.

"Come on," Lola says with a smile as she stands and beckons me toward the table in the corner.

I follow her. I definitely feel plain next to these women who are full of color, glitter and shimmer, but Lola's in her element. She is around the same age as me and I definitely don't consider myself old. In fact, in my profession, I'm still a baby.

When I'm alone with Lola, I'm motherly toward her. I see our mommy/little girl dynamic as clear as day. Although I never before realized that was my thing, it certainly *is* my thing.

But here in Lola's world, it's obvious that Lola is the veteran, the mother hen. The other girls all look at her as she walks over. In a couple of the women, I can see a flash of something like jealousy on their pretty faces. Maybe Lola is a rarity in her field, but most of them have obvious respect, care, and love for her.

"Girls, this is Willow. Willow, these are the girls. They can introduce themselves when they want. You'll forget their names, but that's okay!" she says with a laugh, as she sits down and takes a big drink from her Jack Daniels and coke.

I don't think anyone could necessarily tell they were strippers, but what does strike me is the variety in their appearances. Tall, short, dark, fair, caramel skin, hazel eyes, blonde, full chest, small chest, sweeping hips. Something for every taste.

The one thing they have in common is this easy sensuality, like sex is so natural to them that it seeps out of their every pore. I feel almost turned on by being around women like this.

The bar is buzzing with laughter, music, and the clinking of glasses. Lola and I keep catching each other's eyes from across the table and our eyes hold steady as we sip our drinks.

The girls grow louder as the alcohol flows. They laugh at each other's jokes and share stories of their past experiences. But I only have eyes for Lola, and I feel the sparks flying between us as we lean in closer and closer---the chemistry between us palpable.

As the night wears on, we linger over our drinks and continue flirting, unabated, our bodies inching closer as we bask in each other's company. Finally, we acknowledge our need. With a knowing look, we make the decision to leave the bar together.

Our fingers intertwine as we make our way out of the bar, my heart beating wildly with anticipation. Every moment feels like an eternity as we walk home, the anticipation heightening with every step. The streets are quiet and deserted as we walk arm-in-arm through the empty city. It's three in the morning. Our hair is messy and our faces glow from the drinks we shared at the dive bar.

As we make our way through the cool night air, our conversation becomes hushed and intimate. We share stories and secrets, whispering sweet nothings to each other--our laughter and occasional kisses punctuating the soft sounds of the night. The streetlights cast an ethereal glow on Lola's face, highlighting the want and tenderness that flows between us. And we stop on a quiet street corner, the silence is broken by the sound of our soft kisses and whispered desires to one another.

As we reach my apartment, the air buzzes with electricity. Entering the hallway, we waste no time as we explore each other's bodies. Our passion and chemistry are undeniable. With every touch, kiss, and caress, it's more clear that we have found something special in each other.

9

LOLA

"I don't know what else I can tell you, Pearl," I say. "We haven't really spoken about that stuff. I mean, I just don't think Willow sees her family very much and who am I to ask questions about that, you know?" I lean in closer to the mirror to apply more lipstick, watching Pearl out of the corner of my eye, spinning in her chair as she shrugs.

"I get that, Lola, really I do, but that girl got serious money and just cos she out here hooking up with your delicious ass don't mean she ain't gonna remember that fact sooner or later."

I don't want to roll my eyes at her because I know Pearl is only looking out for me. If I'm the experienced stripper in the group, Pearl is the OG. She doesn't strip anymore, though, as she's closer to the wrong side of fifty. She still works hard. Keeps the ship tight, the girls happy, the liquor ordered, and the place generally well-managed. The good thing about Pearl is that she cares and doesn't talk shit. She shoots as straight as an arrow when she needs to talk to you about having your shit together.

"I know, really I do, Pearl," I say. "But what's a girl gonna do? Willow's hot, sexy, and delicious. She makes me laugh, she turns up, calls me back, and blows my mind when she fucks me. Why make a problem where there isn't one?"

Pearl nods in agreement. "Well, that's a true thing, but just keep your guard up a little, Lola. I ain't ever seen you all up like this, those other girls be fallin' every damn week for some no-good guy, but not you. I don't want you getting hurt, baby girl. Women like Willow don't date strippers."

"I know, Pearl, thanks for caring."

She stands slowly, with a smile.

"Oh, I don't care. I just be thinkin' bout those tips we be missing if we ain't got no Lola on stage!" she says with a wink, as she gives my shoulders a little rub. "You go get em, girl."

And I nod.

I will.

The lights flicker a harsh white strobe that casts shadows over my figure. The spotlight rises and reflects off the black PVC and I know my tanned skin looks pale against it. The contrasts are stark and exaggerated. A contradiction. Just like me.

"*Don't need permission . . .*" I stroll forward, my heels are so high that my instep has to stretch to follow the curve. Latex, pulled tight up my legs, rides the bend of my knee up to my thighs. My one-piece is a work of art. Laced tight at the back,e my waist is drawn in. The PVC skims my hipbones to slip between my thighs, and the boning that supports my chest makes my breasts look enormous. They heave against the plastic with each deep breath I take.

"*All that you got . . . skin to skin . . . Oh my God . . .*" My palms glide over the latex, following the accentuated curves of my waist and moving down between my thighs, where the PVC pulls tight against my sex.

I let myself moan in response to my own touch.

I reach the front as the music climbs. My dark hair is pulled up high into a ponytail and bunny ears are bent on one side, the blend of sexy and cute. My eyes seek out Willow in a sleek blue Armani pantsuit at the bar, looking like she belongs anywhere but here. She's the one I am dancing for. I slowly thrust my hips forward to that deep, low pulse of the beat, hoping she is enjoying the show.

As the dance goes on, I feel more and more turned on. Willow is watching me. She wants me and my dancing is elevated. This performance is real. So real.

"All girls want to be like that . . . Bad girls underneath like that . . ."

As I strip the corset off and my breasts spill out, it feels so good to be free. Cash is being thrown onto the stage and I'm enjoying every last dollar of it.

As we reach the finale and my panties come off, I'm filled with both same thrill I always feel and an extra thrill, just for Willow.

The walk home from the club is always a special time with her. Kisses are exchanged between us, sending shivers down our spines. Our hands thread together, tightening with every step we take. The city buzzes around us, but we are lost in our own world. As we walk, we laugh and whisper secrets to each other, lost in the moment. It is a perfect night; they all are. Slowly blending into each other.

Pearl's words linger in my mind, but when I taste Willow's kisses on my lips, all the warning signs fade away.

Women like her don't date strippers.

How could I doubt that there is anywhere else in this city I'm supposed to be than right here, with her?

10

WILLOW

At seven a.m. sharp, my feet slip into the straps. To anyone else, I am just a woman sweating on an exercise bike in the gym. But in my head, I am escaping, trying not to think about the future. Focusing on the present moment. With each push of the pedals, I can feel my muscles working hard, urging me to peddle faster. Beads of sweat glisten on my forehead as I push myself to my limits. Watching me, you can tell I am not one to give up easily, but right now I feel the waves of uncertainty washing over me.

I'm not worrying about Lola. Lola is the single best thing that happened to me for as long as I can remember.

The dread comes from the upcoming benefit ball tomorrow night. I don't want to go and I would normally not go. But this is the one event that has an actual impact on my career. My boss's boss will be there. And if I know my mother and father, I will be placed right next to this man from the appetizers all the way through to dessert.

I can usually stomach one or two of the fancy events a year, which I have been bred for and trained up for since birth, but my patience has been starting to wear thin in recent years and now things feel different.

Lola just isn't the kind of person that would be accepted or taken seriously in any way, shape, or form as my partner at an event like this--nor in my life in general.

The list of reasons why start with her being female, but that is not by far the most problematic thing about Lola.

There is also the fact that she doesn't come from money. She lives on the wrong side of town. And she takes off her clothes for a living.

Hell, I don't even know Lola's last name. I'm pretty sure she doesn't use one. She is just Lola.

Sure, in polite society, there are eccentrics whom everyone enjoys as entertainment. But they are usually very wealthy women with a penchant for the peculiar. They aren't strippers who come from nothing.

I know I could go to this event by myself and just tell Lola it was a work thing, which would be very honest, and that would be the end of it. She wouldn't question me.

Except . . . that isn't entirely true either.

There are things I hide from Lola.

Lola is a smart woman. I know she intuits that there are vast differences between our lives.

But there are more things I keep from her.

Someone like Lola lives for the moment will never understand why I hide not only my sexuality from the world (which, although once murky, is now suddenly very clear to me: I am a lesbian and I have made peace with that on a personal level) but I also hide who I am from Lola. And I know I will hide her from my family.

Well, I haven't hidden my last name, but Lola doesn't follow politics, either. I'm fairly confident that she hasn't made the connection.

My father aspires to run for president next year. He needs his only daughter to keep being the model senator's daughter she always has been.

A senator's daughter who behaves herself and

keeps her head down. Someone as low profile as it comes.

A senator's daughter who comes out as a lesbian dating a stripper--well, that would be a scandal I'm just not ready for.

Both my and Lola's lives would be dragged into the spotlight.

When I think about what I am keeping from Lola and the fact I don't think I will ever feel okay being open about her, the guilt bubbles up inside me. It feels like I'm choking from within.

How can I ever give Lola what she deserves? How can I offer her a future when she has no clue who I really am? When she does, Lola will know that the chances we have, the actual reality of us being more than this, is pretty much zero.

Lola is my dirty secret. How can I ever tell anyone about us?

This is all my brain speaking. The analyst within me, looking at the situation with logic and the pragmatic viewpoint I'm known for. But another part of me, louder, stronger, and more determined, refuses to listen to that. Deep down inside of me, there is a part that refuses to accept that the best thing in my life is temporary.

I give myself a hard shake and pedal the

workout bike harder and faster. This is why I come here, to *not* think.

If I pedal fast enough, maybe I can shut out all the noise.

I send Lola a text to tell her that I have a work thing. A coward's way out, I know. But I can't see her tonight or tomorrow if I am going to the gala. First, I need to get my hair done, then I have to pick up a ridiculously expensive dress and have every single inch of me poked and prodded so that for one night I can look like I wake up that way— that when you are born this rich, your skin naturally glows in your sleep.

I won't choose the dress; my mother's personal stylist will. She will know what the other big names attending are wearing to be sure that I will appear unique, but still fit in perfectly. She will find the designer name that is just the right one to be wearing now, the shade that is just ahead of the trend, and the cut that will flatter. Something that will be sophisticated and beautiful, while oozing elegance and class.

All I need to do is dash over there after work to make sure the dress is fitted to perfection.

I keep fidgeting with my hands and tapping my foot against the floorboard as we weave through traffic. The driver continues to check his watch, giving me concerned looks in the rearview mirror.

I know he's just trying to be helpful, but it only makes me more anxious. I don't even want to think about what kind of mood my mother is going to be in when she finds out I showed up late to this fitting.

I stare out the window, watching the city rush by in a blur of buildings and people. All I can think about is how much I'd rather be anywhere else. But I know there's no escaping this appointment. As we pull up to the boutique, my heart sinks. I take a deep breath and step out of the cab, steeling myself for whatever comes next. It's time to face the music and get this over with.

Shona is cool. She is unemotional regarding my tardiness, which suits me perfectly. I know Shona will just add an extra charge onto my mother's bill, and that suits us both. I can barely summon any excitement as I walk into Shona's dress-fitting studio, but she should know by now not to expect excitement from me over dresses.

While I can almost get excited over a beautifully fitted pant suit, dresses just seem to stress me out. There is so much pressure for them to be just right. For my body in the dress to be just right. Shona greets me with a lukewarm smile and ushers me to the dressing room.

As she helps me into the stunning silver dress, I can't help but feel like it's a royal waste of time. It will look like every other other dress I've worn a million times. And then I see myself in the mirror.

The way the fabric drapes over my curves is simply breathtaking. It hugs all the right places and flows gracefully down to the floor. I gasp at how beautiful I look. It is a dress that could truly steal the show.

The classic style exudes elegance and sophistication, and the color complements my skin tone perfectly. It's as if this dress was made just for me.

I twirl and admire the way the material sways with every movement. Shona watches with pride, knowing she has found the perfect dress for me. "Always so little faith," she says, as if she had known my thoughts when I first got here. "And I won't tell your mother you were late," she adds with a little smirk as she starts to unpin me. I give her a smile. Maybe she is one of the good ones after all.

I arrive at the gala, feeling uneasy and out of place--not that I don't belong, but rather that I don't <u>want</u> to belong to this world anymore. I force a smile as I step out of the car alone, surrounded by flashy cars and people dressed in ridiculously expensive clothing. My mother had suggested a list of suitable men I should contact as my plus-one for the evening, but I just couldn't face it this time. The thought of a man on my arm and an evening of pretense makes me feel sick now.

I mentally add that to my list of *things my mother is not going to be happy about.*

The grand entrance to the gala is overwhelming, with bright lights and decorations that sparkle like diamonds. My mother has really gone to town this time.

I'm used to such extravagance and luxury but it still makes me feel icky and uncomfortable. Still, this event is important for me to attend. As I make my way inside, everyone turns their heads to look at me. Here, I am. No longer Willow, but Senator

Rutherford's daughter, which is both a blessing and a curse.

I feel exposed, even though I'm dressed beautifully. But despite how uncomfortable I feel, I try to hold my head high and appear confident. It seems like everyone there has someone to talk to except me. Which makes me a prime target for small talk.

As I make my way through the crowd, older men keep trying to chat and flirt with me. They talk about themselves and their accomplishments, clearly thinking they are impressing me. But all I can think about is how bored and uncomfortable I feel. I try to politely excuse myself from each encounter, but they just won't take a hint. It's exhausting.

I avoid my parents as much as possible, which is not easy. My radar is on full alert for them. I'm moving through the event seamlessly, never lingering in one place for too long. Making sure I take my seat at the last minute so I couldn't get the "Willow darling" drop-by my mother loves to do. I settle in my seat, unfolding my napkin over my lap and glancing around the table.

Of course, I'm seated at the same table as my boss.

As soon as he sits down next to me, his

charming presence makes me feel a bit more comfortable. He starts asking about my life outside of work and I find myself opening up to him. He is a nice guy--not what I expected. He is respectful in his questions, while pushing deeper to find out more from me.

I can see how impressed my boss is with my achievements and success. But deep down, I can't help but wonder if this is all just for show. Does he really care about me, or is he just trying to get on my good side because of who my father is?

Either way, I know that making a good impression on my boss tonight is important for my career. So I play along and engage him in conversation throughout the night. Despite my reservations, I can't deny that being in his company makes the evening slightly more bearable. Maybe, just maybe, this night isn't such a waste after all.

But eventually, I can't take it anymore. I find an excuse to leave early and practically run out the door, relieved to escape the stifling atmosphere. As the cab takes me away, I realize that money can buy many things, but it can never buy genuine human connection or happiness. And that thought makes me lean forward to tell the driver that my destination has changed. I need to go to where I really want to be: asleep in Lola's arms.

I stumble into her apartment, tired and slightly tipsy from the wine that helped me survive the night. I can tell she is confused. It is Lola's night off, so she has been resting for a while. She is already bleary-eyed and half asleep as I strip off my gown. She eyes it suspiciously and I know I am going to get questions about it tomorrow. I climb into bed next to Lola. I pull her up close and tight to me. I feel the need rise in her, to touch and to please me, but I stop her.

"I want you to fall asleep. Deep asleep in my arms. And then wake up to me," I say. "I want you to know how it feels to wake up as my needy girl. Will you do that for me?" I ask Lola softly, as I wrap her up and play with her beautiful long hair. She nods, looking straight into my eyes as she does.

"I really want that."

When Lola is really asleep, I put my hand on her head. I take my time gently guiding her down my body. She stirs a little, and I slow my pace until she is curled up warm between my thighs, her cheek gently resting against my pussy. She doesn't even know I have put her there because she has slept through it, but now Lola can smell me in her sleep, and I like that.

Soon the efforts of the evening overcome me and I fall asleep myself.

I wake up to Lola nuzzling against my pussy. As I look down, I see that she is still half asleep. I reach down and open myself slightly for her. And as though on instinct, Lola's mouth opens and her tongue reaches for me. I let out a sigh.

When she does wake, she will be surrounded by me. Her first everything will be me.

I start to rock more against her mouth. Small movements, but enough to make her body move too. I want her to wake up to me. I want to feel that pause as she stirs and tries to understand where she is. And then as she realizes . . . she'll just settle in and lick more and more.

Slowly, Lola starts to wake.

I can see her eyelids flicker open. Her body tenses a little as that confusion flashes through her, as she tries to make sense of it all.

I stroke her hair the way I always do, soft and gentle, conditioning her body to know it's okay.

That she doesn't need to think. She just needs to do whatever I want.

The moment passes and she reaches with her tongue again, settling immediately into licking me.

I let out a deeper sigh. Her tongue swirls as I feel her early morning hunger and her constant need for me. She has no shame or reluctance to show how much she wants me. Just eager, hungry licks, again and again.

I want to be her last taste every night and her first taste every morning.

My legs wrap around her. Sometimes I let her have space to explore and enjoy. But right now I need pressure. I need to grind against her pretty face.

She seems to sense what I want and pushes her face into me. Again and again in between licks. She knows what I want, and she gives it to me. She only wants to make me feel good.

"Fuck . . . ." I pull her in harder. My hips push up toward her. It makes me feel so good knowing that she has woken up like this. Minutes ago, Lola was asleep and now she is such a needy, desperate good girl, doing exactly what I want.

"You are such a good girl . . . such a good fucking girl . . ." I tell her over and over through my moans. Sometimes she can't hear me because my thighs are so tight around her. But she knows. She can feel it. She can taste how good she is, all for me.

When I press her face tight into me it shuts everything out, and for once the noise in my head is quiet and I can lose myself in the feeling.

Her eyes are closed and I watch her lovely dark eyelashes flicker between my legs in concentration. Her face looks so beautiful, even there. Especially there.

I grind myself against her until I'm shaking hard. And Lola knows my body so well now. She knows what it means, so she presses her face in more.

And I let it happen. I let it build until it is all I can do, coming loud and hard all over her tongue and face. I fall back, my legs opening as I release her from my grip. But she still licks and laps until I can't take anymore and then I reach for her. Pulling her up to me, so I can touch and taste her in return. Repaying the gift because she was such a good girl for me. My good girl.

11
LOLA

The previous day I had woken up late, feeling groggy and a bit disoriented. After rubbing my eyes for a few seconds, I remembered that it was my day off from work at the club.

I rolled over in bed, staring up at the ceiling for a moment as I contemplated what to do with my free time. Eventually, I decided that I could use a good cup of coffee and some window shopping, so I got dressed and headed into the city.

As I walked through the busy streets, taking in all the sights and sounds around me, something nagged at the back of my mind. Willow had been acting a little distant lately and I couldn't shake the feeling that something was wrong between us.

I tried to push those thoughts aside and focus on enjoying my day out, but they kept creeping back in, no matter how hard I tried to ignore them. Finally, after browsing through a few stores and sipping on my latte, I decided to call her and see if everything was okay.

Willow answered after a few rings, sounding surprised to hear from me. We chatted for a few minutes about nothing in particular before I finally mustered up the courage to ask her what was going on. She reassured me instantly that she was just busy--a stupid work thing tonight. That she really couldn't get out of and really didn't want to go to. I felt it in her voice, could hear the honesty and frustration. I let that settle my doubts. "Well, you can end up at my place anytime, if you want. I am not at work later," I tell her.

As I stepped inside my small, one-bedroom apartment, the mess overwhelmed me. The dirty dishes were piled up in the sink, the clothes scattered around on the floor, and dust was on every surface.

I took a deep breath, put on some music, and got to work. With each dish I cleaned, each shirt folded, and each piece of trash thrown away, I felt more accomplished. My efforts were paying off as my tiny living space began to transform into a tidy sanctuary.

I kept going until everything was spotless, even taking time to rearrange furniture for a fresh, new look. When I was finally done, I stood back to admire my hard work. A smile spread across my face. It might have been a small victory, but it was still an achievement that brought me peace of mind.

I plopped down on my bed, feeling satisfied and content. It's amazing how much better I feel when my surroundings are clean and organized. Plus, now I would able to relax without any nagging guilt about having left chores undone.

It got later and later and I didn't hear anything from Willow. Not even a text. I knew she was busy with her work thing, but I couldn't help but feel a little down about it.

I don't usually sleep early on my nights off because it just throws me off the next day, but I was so tired that I got into bed. I felt like I had only been there a few seconds when I heard Willow at the door, letting herself in with the key from under the mat.

Still half asleep, I watched her--unfocused as she appeared in the doorway. Still, I couldn't help but notice what she was wearing. Expensive, fitted, named, couture—that dress was probably worth more than my entire wardrobe put together. But I couldn't focus because Willow was taking everything off and she looked stunning. She looked like she had stepped out of a magazine. And I could smell her. I needed Willow so much that I couldn't think.

"I want you to fall asleep. Deep asleep in my arms. And then wake up to me," she says. "I want you to know how it feels to wake up being my needy girl. Will you do that for me?" she asks, as I look up into her eyes. The second she says it, I want it. I need it.

"I really want that," I say.

And I do. And then we do. We wake up like that and I dive into it. I let myself feel all of the emotions that come when I am in that head space with her. Letting my body be a slave to her every desire. It makes me feel so good to do it. I am like an addict, needing and wanting more and more of her.

After catching my breath and waking up a little more, I realize that I'm a little sore and still disoriented. And my body aches. I pull myself out of bed and stumble into the kitchen. I need some coffee to help me focus.

I start brewing a fresh pot and try to remember how Willow and I ended up in bed together. It's all a bit hazy, but I know it was intense and amazing. My mind drifts back to the feel of her skin on mine, the sound of her moans, and the taste of her lips.

But then something else catches my attention: the dress she was wearing last night. It looks like something a famous actress might wear to the Oscars.

"Willow, do you want coffee?" I call, even though she is only ten feet away from me. My apartment is smaller than her walk-in closet, but she still surprises me--standing in the doorframe in one of my long shirts, with smeared makeup and messy golden hair. Looking so fucking sexy.

"I would love one," she says with a seductive smile, and I move to get her a mug.

"So . . . where were you last night again?" I ask.

I time my question to coincide with the moment I look up from the cup, so I can see her reaction. I don't think Willow is dating anyone else and I don't think she would come home to me after a date with another person. But I also know that we haven't had that conversation yet, and that is a really, really expensive dress.

"I was at a work gala thing," she says. "I didn't want to go. I wanted to be here with you, but I had to make an appearance. I thought I could slide in and out pretty fast, but I had been seated at the table with my boss. Well, my boss's boss. Which meant I really had to make sure I made a good impression. So I stayed until it wasn't rude to leave."

I study Willow. She is honest in what she is saying, but my spidey senses are still tingling.

"And did you?" I ask as I slide her mug over.

"Did I what?" she asks, a little confused. Another clue that she isn't quite telling me everything.

"Make a good impression?"

She relaxes. "Oh, I mean, sure. I think so." She takes a sip. "I mean, it isn't going to make any difference right now. But all these things help in the long run. Networking."

I nod. "Did you take a date?" I ask it casually, but she looks at me incredulously, shocked.

"A date? No. Why would I take a date?" she asks.

I shrug. "I don't know. That is a very special dress. You are a very special woman. It seems a shame for you to be there dateless."

Willow steps forward, placing her cup on the counter as she makes her way around to me. Her hands are on me, wrapping around me. One up into my hair and the other down onto my lower back. "Lola . . . I think if I were going to take a date, I would make sure it was with the girl I am falling in love with. Wouldn't you?"

I pause a second and my whole body tenses. I feel Willow's words wash over me.

The girl I am falling in love with.

Funny, how it can take someone else to say something, for you to realize your own feelings.

I love her too.

I nod slowly. "I think that would be a good idea, Willow. Also, a good idea to tell the girl, too. That you felt that way. So she knew."

"I think that would be a good idea. You are right." She pulls away seriously before taking my face in her palms. She tilts my chin up just an inch, even though we are nearly the same height. She looks me straight in the eyes, seriously, honestly. Her eyes are glowing amber in the light.

"Lola. You are the best thing that has happened to me in a really, really long time. Maybe even ever. The times I'm with you are the happiest I have ever been. And I am very much falling in love with you."

And then she turns my face toward hers and gently presses her lips against mine. I never thought that a kiss could feel like this. So soft, so gentle, and so full of love. I feel safe, protected, and adored.

Our kiss isn't rushed or aggressive, or even sexual. It is just pure, innocent, and loving. Our lips dance together and we explore each other's mouths, without needing to go any further than that.

I can feel my heart beating faster as our kiss continues. My body is reacting instinctively to the warmth and tenderness shared between us. I know in that moment that I want to spend the rest of my life with this woman.

Eventually, we break apart, both of us gasping for air, but smiling from ear to ear. We look into each other's eyes and know that what we have is real. As we stand there holding each other, basking in the afterglow of our gentle kiss, I know that I will not forget this moment anytime soon.

Willow and I decide to spend some time outside. It is Saturday, and it's not that often I get out in the daylight. I just can't believe how lucky I am to be sitting here with Willow. The sun is shining down on us as we laugh and flirt while enjoying our ice cream in the park. Her perfect smile lights up the entire area, making everything feel brighter and happier.

We talk about all sorts of things, from our favorite movies to the best places we've traveled. It feels like we could sit here forever, just talking and laughing together.

As we finish our ice cream, Willow looks at me with those beautiful amber eyes and tells me softly, "I'm having such a great time with you." My heart skips a beat as I realize that I feel the exact same way.

I reach for her hand and give it a gentle squeeze, feeling the warmth and softness of her skin against mine. I gaze into Willow's eyes for what feels like an eternity. We are lost in our own little world.

Finally, she leans in and kisses me softly on the lips. My whole body tingles with excitement as we embrace, wrapped up in each other's arms. I pull her closer, not wanting to let go. Her touch is electric and I can't get enough.

Willow's tongue tastes of vanilla and I wonder if she can taste the strawberry on mine. And as a couple walk past us with a loud tut and a sigh. I pull back away, remembering where I am, and we both start to giggle.

"You have me feeling like a teenage girl, Willow."

"I just wanted a taste of your ice cream." She grins and I give her a playful tap on her thighs.

"Also, I just realized I don't know anything about your family." I ask the question I realize we have both been hiding from for a while now.

Something like panic momentarily flashes across her beautiful face, but she hides it well.

"You don't?!" she gasps, playfully. "Well, guess what, Ms. Lola?"

"What?" I say with a smile, playing the game too.

"I don't even know your last name, so I guess we both have our secrets."

I laugh and lean back in for another kiss, sealing our secrets, although I think to myself that mine isn't much of a good secret at all.

12

WILLOW

It is funny how slowly time can pass when things seem gray, then how they can flash by in the blink of an eye when someone brings a multitude of colors that make every day sparkle with new shades and perspectives.

Love. Not something I ever thought I would find. It is like a warm embrace, filling my heart with joy and making me smile from ear to ear. I feel like I'm walking on air--as if nothing can bring me down. This magical sensation makes me believe in forever, in a happily ever after. Lola is the best thing that has ever happened to me.

But she doesn't know who I am.

I mean that isn't strictly true. She *does* know

who I am. Lola knows me better than anyone has ever known me or could possibly know me. But Lola doesn't know where I come from. She doesn't understand the implications of being with me.

"Lola, I want to take all my clothes off and feel you all over me," I say.

"Yeah? What should I start with, baby?"

I take off my socks and walk over to her, putting my foot on her thigh. "My toes."

Lola takes my foot and gently runs her fingers along the bottom. Pressing, a soft massage.

It makes me gasp a little. My muscles tense, then slowly I relax with each press of her fingers. Then I switch, giving her the other foot. Wanting the same touches.

Willow gives the same attention to that foot. Then she brings it up a little and bends her head down to give my toes a kiss before continuing the massage.

My fingers reach and gently run through Lola's soft, dark hair. Petting her as she gives me a kiss. It feels so sweet and soft, and her fingers move so well against my foot and toes. I start to work down my yoga pants, slowly, lifting my foot to slip them free.

She helps me pull them the rest of the way off, and then she goes back down to my foot to give my toes another kiss.

"I like that, baby," I tell her softly, praising Lola for doing such a good job and making me feel so special. "You can touch me a little higher. More kisses, baby." I lift my foot, holding the top of her head to steady myself as I rest it on her shoulder, so now my calf rests against her cheek.

She turns and starts to press her lips up further. She lets her tongue drag up my leg as her hands also trail behind to squeeze, press, and massage all over the new spaces.

My hand stays on top of her head, keeping me balanced as she touches and kisses me. It feels so good. I slowly lower my foot back down, standing between her thighs as she sits on the couch. And I softly tell her, "Take off my panties, baby."

Lola slowly reaches her hands up my legs until she gets to my hips. Her fingers hook into my panties and she slowly and softly pulls them down my body.

I start to stroke her hair before tilting her head back. Now she is looking up at me as I draw her in.

Her chin rests against my pelvis. "You remember that video we watched . . . how good she licked? How hungry . . . eager . . . desperate she was?"

Lola bites her lip and nods slowly.

I keep stroking her hair, pressing a little harder against her. So close. She is just so close to my pussy. "Do you think you can lick like that?"

She nods again slowly before whispering, "Yes."

My fingers keep running through Lola's hair, brushing it back as I look down into her big, blue eyes. She's so needy, so desperate to please. "I think you would try so hard," I say. "Wouldn't you, baby?"

"Yes. Your pussy is the only thought I have. The only thing I want. The only thing I need."

I don't part my thighs. I don't do anything to help her. Lola will have to work for it. She will have to show me just how much she wants it, needs it. And I know she will. I know it is all she can think about as I give her one last slow pet. "Show me."

She starts to kiss up my thighs. Hungry, needy, full kisses. Her hands cling to the backs of my thighs and I can feel her hands gripping, holding onto me. It is so fucking sexy. Surely Lola can feel me tremble and shiver as my feet slowly start to spread, parting my thighs at the same time hers do. Lola's face inches teasingly closer, and then she is there. Pressed right to me. She takes a quick lick. And then another. A kiss. And then another. Like each one could be her last.

My feet slide together a bit, my thighs closing again, but this time her face is there. Lola is trapped slightly between my legs as she holds me. Quick licks come first, but they grow with each taste she is getting--an addict getting her fix and only wanting more and more.

She presses her face right against me. As tight as she can get it because she needs to be that close to my pussy. She needs to inhale it, to let it fill her up, and to press her tongue to it. Her licks get longer, still maintaining that level of need, desire, and hunger she has for me. She lets out a moan against me and a shiver because it is just so good.

"Fuck." I feel it. Lola makes me feel how much she needs it and wants it. And the wetter I get, the more I feel, the more she gives, until she is moaning and shivering. All for me. Not even touching herself. Just being able to taste me and make me feel good makes her tremble. It is so intoxicating to watch her like this.

Her hands are still on my thighs, clinging as

she continues to drag her tongue over and over. She presses it with the hunger she feels and her need to make me feel so good.

"Fuck, baby . . ." My voice trails off. Lola has been like this since the second she opened her eyes. Wearing my scent. Desperate to please. And she is pleasing me. Fuck, she is making me feel so good.

I start to move forward, rocking into her. I am shaking hard and it's difficult to stay standing. But her hands just grip me tighter, holding me in place so she can keep licking. So much pressure. Looking down and watching her bury her face in me, I don't even know how she can breathe. We are so tight together, and it all just feels so good. I grip her hair, resting the other hand on the wall behind her because I'm about to lose my battle to stay upright. I'm about to orgasm. So hard. All over her.

"I need it so bad," she whispers against me.

"You are going to have it. Fuck! I am going to . . ."

I can't keep talking. I push Lola back further on the couch, following her there on my knees. Her hands pull my ass tight against her, keeping me spread against her. I'm grinding myself all over her, wet smears over her face. I am so sensitive. I

13
LOLA

It is finally starting to get old.

I wondered if it would ever wane, my love for the job.

Pearl told me once that everyone tires of it eventually, and it seems that time is coming for me.

I stare into the mirror, letting out a sigh. I still look the part and I know the dances inside out. I love the atmosphere, the place, and the people . . . but stripping itself is starting to lose its appeal. I have been doing it for so long that when I think about it, I don't even know who Lola is without a pole.

"You're up," Pearl calls from the doorway. "And no, she ain't here. She said she will meet you after."

I nod, but I'm sad that Willow won't be in the crowd. It's my favorite thing, to see her at the bar. But I'm happy she'll be with me afterward, during the walk back to her place and then those beautiful egyptian cotton sheets.

The curtains open to reveal a stage that's a replica of a nineties high school classroom. Little wooden tables lined up, chalkboard covered in smears and white dust, the clock counting down to the bell. I sit, tapping my pencil.

Then I stand slowly, big eyes wide and innocent. My hair is up in loose pigtails and a smear of sticky pink gloss makes my lips shine. My uniform pushes the dress code, but isn't that what rules are for, to break? It's a little black skirt with tiny pleats that barely cover my ass, a crisp white shirt tied at my waist, and a tie that only exists to draw attention to how many buttons I don't have fastened.

I stand slowly, black socks covering my legs up to my knees. The folded pleats skim the tops of my thighs, barely covering my panties as I step in front of my desk. My hands rest on the edge and I sit there as I look up at the crowd from under my long lashes.

"My loneliness is killing me . . ." My fingers drop

to my waist, toying with the knot in my shirt, pulling at the fabric until it comes undone. *"When I'm not with you, I lose my mind..."* I bunch the fabric up in my hands and give a hard pull, feeling the buttons ping open. *"Hit me, baby, one more time."*

I shrug my shoulders, my shirt dropping to the floor. My breasts spill from my tight little black bra and my tie rests between the mounds of flesh, drawing the audience's gaze as they bounce with every slow step I take. My fingers slip the knot so that the tie is only resting around my neck. My palms splay out on the table in front of me.

"Show me how you want it to be..." My hands slide forward, my shoulders together so that my breasts squeeze, a hint of nipple peaking from the top of my bra. My neck rolls, stretched out, craving the drag of Willow's tongue. Imagining her taking a taste of me before she leaves her mark. I let out a soft moan.

"My loneliness is killing me..." My nails skim down my stomach, toying with the edge of my skirt, hips slowly rolling as I tease the skirt down. *"When I'm not with you, I lose my mind..."* My fingers skim over my panties, revealing the black silk inch by inch. *"Hit me, baby, one more time..."* I

finish my walk to the front of the stage, letting out a long, slow sigh as I drop to my knees.

The lights drop, but a single spotlight remains on me, lighting up my skin as I kneel on display.

"*I must confess . . . my loneliness . . .*" I look up. My eyes search for her, even though know she isn't there. My soul bared, I feel a longing ache for her. My fingers run up the lower part of my spine. A quick flick at the clasp of my bra, a roll of my shoulders, and the soft black satin drops. My nipples harden on show, desperate for a soothing suck, wanting the feel of her on me.

"*Hit me baby one more time.*" My knees slide wide and my palms rest on the stage in front of me. Between my thighs. The neediness takes over, my hips dropping low, my thighs tensing as my body moves into a soft, aching grind against the floor. A touch, her touch, is all I need and want--but this is all I can take.

"*I must confess . . . my loneliness . . . is killing me now . . .*" I plead for her, feeling a tingle running through me as my pussy drags across the floor, finally a touch where I long for it most. And I let out a whimper. Feeling wetness soak through the satin, a creamy smear of lust for her. I fall back, knees parted, thighs in a wide V, pussy tight against black silk. I know the front row can see the outline of my femininity. "*Hit me baby one more time.*" And the stage goes black. I'm dazed by my own performance for a moment before I make my way back to the dressing room.

"You just get better and better, Lola. Your tips will be huge tonight." I look up to see Landon in the doorway.

I grin. "I didn't realize you watched me."

He gives a shrug. "I like watching the things I want, but can't have. Keeps me humble."

I raise an eyebrow. "You are not humble . . . And you don't want some old stripper like me."

He laughs. "Oh, Lola, if only you knew the truth, darlin'. But anyway, I've been nervous. Saw you with that rich girl more and more. Figured I was about to lose you. Then you put on a show like that. You really are the best. I've put in a little extra for you. Like I said, I like watching."

I ponder Landon's comments as I head out, thinking about how I had felt before my dance. The truth is . . . I have been thinking of getting out of the business. The only reason I put on a show like that was because I'm achy for Willow. Pining for her like I do whenever we have to spend more than twenty-four hours apart. She's in my heart, my head, and my panties constantly. I have a desperate need that only Willow can fill. The second I see her outside the club, I pounce on her. I cover her in kisses and wrap her up close to me.

"Well, hey to you too," she says with a smile, breathless but glowing. "What was that for?"

"No reason," I say, threading my arm through hers and holding her close. "I just missed you." I give her a smile.

"I missed you too, baby girl, but I have some bad news," she says.

I feel my heart sink. "What is it?" I ask softly, and she squeezes me tight.

"I can't show you how much I've missed you for another hour because we need to walk past the office. I left my purse in my drawer."

I let out an audible sigh of relief. "I can wait an hour. Just barely, I think."

I hold her hand tightly as we walk through the quiet streets, our laughter echoing in the night. It is late, but that doesn't matter to us. We're lost in each other's company, enjoying every moment.

As we approach Willow's office building, I can't

help but feel a sense of nervousness creeping up inside me. The world can be so judgmental sometimes. I worry about what people might say or think about us. Willow carefully releases my hand and gives me a kiss on the cheek. "I will only be two minutes, okay? I can't let you in. I'd get in trouble . . ." Her voice trails off and I nod, completely understanding. It's a government site with limited access. I can wait.

I stand outside the towering office building, surrounded by the darkness of the night. My heart beats with anticipation as I anxiously wait for my lover to join me outside. The city lights shimmer in the distance, casting a warm glow on the streets below.

I can't help but feel a mixture of excitement and nervousness coursing through my veins. Every passing minute feels like an eternity, as I long for her. Thoughts of our last time together dance in my mind, igniting a fire within me that can only be quenched by her touch.

As I glance up at the imposing building, its windows seem to hold secrets untold. What decisions are made behind those walls? What kind of power was wielded there? It's a place where dreams are shaped and destinies altered, yet here I am, waiting patiently in the shadows for her embrace.

She comes out in a rush and it only takes me a few seconds to bound over to her. Wrapping my arms around her again as she giggles. Stumbling into the shadows with me, kissing me back. Until she stops and freezes like a block of ice.

"Willow?" The voice cuts through the dark like a blade of ice. I have no idea who the woman is-- older, expensive, and dripping in couture. But then I can see the resemblance as she steps into the light. And I know, instantly.

"Mom," Willow replies with a pained whisper. She suddenly sounds eight years old.

And with that one word, I know that everything is about to change.

14

WILLOW

I could have blamed my misfortune on complacency. If only I'd been stricter with myself about the affection I showed Lola in public. If only I had called my mom back, instead of dodging her calls a thousand times. If I had just picked up my purse instead of rushing out the door from work... If, if, if.

But the real answer is that if I had just told Lola the truth, none of this would have happened. If I'd had the courage to be who I really am, well then, things most definitely would have played out differently.

But of all the things I wish I could change about that moment, it was hearing my name, spoken in that tone. It took me back to a privileged mindset I wish I could erase from my brain. As I pulled away from Lola in that second, I looked at her—and I mean I <u>looked</u> at her, through the privileged Rutherford eyes I had grown up with. I saw Lola's cheap outfit, her thick makeup, her messy hair with its home dye job, and the fake jewelry. Then I saw her big, hurt, blue eyes, seeing how I looked at her. Understanding in an instant because Lola knows me better than anyone. Seeing how I can change in a second to a person she doesn't know and wouldn't want to know. A person that I hated. And suddenly I couldn't look at Lola. The pain in her lovely, trusting eyes hurt me too much. I turned away from her and greeted my reality.

"Mom."

15
GRACIE

Gracie Rutherford was a rare breed in the city's prestigious social circles. First, she hadn't married into money; she was born with it. And not just money, but class. A history that could be traced back to British high society, which meant she knew her Ps and Qs perfectly and her tea from her teas. Secondly, Gracie Rutherford hadn't married below her social status. Jackson Rutherford, Jr. had some clout when it came to pedigree, fourth-generation wealth—long enough to be considered old money by American standards. Plus he had a bank balance that made hers seem like pocket money. Thirdly, the couple lived impeccably by the rules of their standings. There would be no dirt found on Gracie Rutherford. Not a single smear.

Gracie had supported Jackson in his career as a Senator, but that wasn't the end of her ambitions. She had her sights set on the White House and she knew it was a realistic next step for them.

Her children, however, had posed some problems. Two boys so close together in age that they competed all the time, but they also lacked direction. It took a considerable amount of background management to get them where they needed to be. It was a work in progress, but Gracie had the time to make it her priority. After all, those boys would be her legacy.

Her daughter posed a different issue entirely. On paper, Willow Rutherford was the perfect child, growing into the perfect polite girl and then into a perfect, high-achieving, beautiful woman. But life was not all on paper. Willow was distant, cold, and unforgiving. Every decision her father made was questioned, every social event Gracie arranged was pushed back on, and the relationship between mother and daughter was fractious and filled with contempt.

But just like with her sons, Gracie wasn't about to quit. Willow just needed to find the right man who was part of the right circle. Then she would see just how perfect life could, and would, be for her.

Except that this kind of good management required Willow to take Gracie's calls, and over the past six months, this had barely happened at all. Gracie had seen Willow only once during that time, at a gala Willow was absolutely required to attend for her career, and which she had worked so hard for. But even then, Willow was in and out without a single word to Gracie or her father.

Gracie had done some snooping, and as far as she could tell, nothing was amiss. Work was still Willow's focus, according to the glowing reports from above. Friends said she was happier, she kept all her fitness appointments, and the doctor assured Gracie that Willows's annual check-up had come back as it should. She was a perfectly healthy woman of her age.

But something was different. The distance between mother and daughter had become a chasm, and Gracie wasn't prepared to let it go on any longer.

She wouldn't ambush Willow at work. That could create an unsavory scene, which would be no good for anyone. So instead, Gracie had asked the security guard there to give her a call when Willow left the office alone late one night. Then she could start her "happenstance" meeting, with no cynical looks from her sometimes-too-smart-for-her-own-good daughter.

There was a dark-haired woman loitering nearby in a cheap, too-short skirt. Gracie noticed her the same way you might notice anything else that didn't warrant your attention. A quick scan, an assessment, and then forgotten. That was, until Willow came out of the building and went running to her.

Gracie knew the look on Willow's face. It was love. Romantic idealism and the hope that the world wouldn't taint this love. That this love of hers was forever.

But love was not on Gracie's agenda for Willow. Willow was supposed to be marrying suitably--for everything <u>except</u> love.

Love clouds what is important in life, Gracie knew. She would never give into something as pointless as love herself.

She screwed her face up in disgust. Willow was kissing the girl. The girl who looked like some kind of low-class hooker.

Gracie's voice came out steely, the same tone

she used when they had misbehaved as children. When they had been caught in the act. She didn't show the shock or surprise she felt at Willow kissing this woman, just the cool, authoritative tone of a mother chastising her child.

Gracie saw the world crumble in Willows's eyes as she turned, and she had a feeling in her stomach that the chasm between them may have just split wide open.

16: Willow

The rest happened in a blur. Detaching from Lola, told her I needed to go--not meeting her eyes as she asks if I will call her later. Not meeting my mother's eyes as she ushers me into the luxury, chauffeured car.

The silence was not merely deafening. It was suffocating and I felte like I could choke on it. That the silence could swallow me whole. Then I wished it would, so that I could escape the nightmare of what was about to come. It took a few minutes becaues my mom's brain was on overdrive. I could almost hear the mental checklist she was running through on how to limit the potential shame I could cause her. Then the questions started. They were matter-of-fact. Cold and detached, more like a lawyer than a mother.

"How long has it been going on?" she bit out.

"Six or seven months."

"How did you meet?"

"A strip club."

"Does anyone know?" By "anyone," Mom meant anyone important.

"No."

"Does she know who you are?" In other words, who my father is.

"No."

"What is her name?"

"Lola."

"Lola...?"

"Just Lola."

At that, she gives a cold laugh. "Like the showgirl."

"Exactly. She is a stripper, her name is Lola, she works in a strip club. She doesn't follow politics. She has no idea who I am, or who the Rutherfords are. Nobody you know knows Lola. She isn't after my money and she isn't a bad person. None of this has anything to do with her, so leave her out of it before you start judging her."

My mom bristles beside me. "Willow, you are

very naive and stupid to think she has nothing to do with any of this. If she did know who you are, it would only be a matter of time before she asks for money. The fact that she doesn't know who you are only means we can pinpoint the exact moment she *will* ask for money—the second she finds out."

I turn to my mother angrily. "You don't know a single thing about her, and you have no idea what kind of person she is. But I can tell you, under no uncertain terms, that she would never ask for money. And where are we going? Why are we going to the house? Just take me home. I don't need an intervention. It is my life, goddamn it, and I am not going to be told how to live it by you." I start to tap on the glass to get the driver's attention, but he studiously ignores me.

"If you are quite finished with your tantrum, you should know that he can't hear you. I like to feel sure that my private conversations are just that. You may think I don't know that girl, but I know a thousand like her. A pretty face and some big boobs. While I thought I would need to keep that kind of trash away from your brothers, I never . . . well . . ." Her voice trails off as if she isn't at all prepared to acknowledge that I am actually gay. "Anyway. You will come back to the house, Willow, because there are things to be done. You tell me, Willow, how hard is it for a woman to achieve the success you are aiming for? How many women have held that job? I'll tell you- zero." She turns to look me straight in the face.

"And tell me how your already near-impossible chance for success would be affected if it became public that you are in a relationship with a female stripper who goes by only one name. You'd be without your own surname to fall back on, without my social reach, without your daddy's money, and without every single thing this world has ever given you to succeed--other than that stubborn head of yours that tells you that you are better than me and your father. You have never needed us and you never will . . . but you still keep using the very things we have given you to succeed in life." She lets out a frustrated sigh, sitting back in her seat. Angry at herself for the outburst of emotion.

"Yes, you will come back to the house, Willow. And we are going to clean up this mess once and for all. Let me tell you: after tonight, your daddy and I never want to hear that showgirl's name again."

I feel the tears run down my face. I have spent

my entire life focused on one goal. One job. One seat. I can get there. I know in my heart and head that I can do it. But never without them. It was why I put up with the rest of it, for that goal. To get there.

My mother's threat is real, the implication loud and clear. Go to the house and let Mommy and Daddy fix my silly little mess for me, or go to my apartment. Back to a life with Lola. And kiss goodbye every single dream I had had before I met her.

I nod. Words are difficult but the tears won't stop. It's a constant stream of despair.

My mom reaches for my hand. She's not a cold woman; she does love me. She just doesn't understand me because I don't want the life she wants for me.

My heart is broken.

"It will heal," she says softly, barely a whisper.

I don't reply because I know it never will.

16
LOLA

The week that followed was perhaps the longest and darkest of my life.

I had known there was something hiding under the surface when it came to Willow. I had never felt like Willow was keeping a secret from me. Instead, I'd felt like she hadn't found the right moment to share all of herself yet. And I was okay with that because I thought we had forever.

I could have looked her up on Google. I know I could have. I knew that it would have given me the answers.

But I had chosen to respect Willow's privacy. Sharing was something to be earned, not just taken.

But after the two-line break-up text I got, I guessed that Google was now fair game.

'Willow Rutherford," I typed with a desperate twist deep in my stomach.

Google held nothing back.

Willow Elizabeth Rutherford. Daughter of Senator Jackson Rutherford Jr.

Of course. Why had I not connected her name to his? When I looked at his photo next to hers, I could see the same strong nose and hazel eyes with flecks of amber.

Willow Rutherford. The senator's daughter.

A woman like her doesn't date strippers, Lola.

Her life had been documented via magazines I would never read. Her family was splashed across pages and pages of who's who. Photos of Willow on yachts with billionaires and at the Hamptons with A-list celebrities. Interview articles where her father's unscrupulous business decisions were questioned, and Willow's stoic, no-comment responses. The preppy schools, the studies abroad, and even a college with had her last name on half the buildings on campus.

I knew Willow. My Willow. But Willow Elizabeth Rutherford, Senator Rutherford's daughter, was a stranger to me.

Still, I held on tight. I understood exactly what had happened. She hadn't wanted to tell me in case it changed things, which it would have. How could it not?

And if Willow had told me, then we would have had to confront the inevitable question of what was going on between us. And where could it possibly lead.

Women like her don't date women like me.

She hadn't told her parents because . . . well. We all know why. Then suddenly Willow's world was upended, so she retreated and hid from who she really is.

All that I could understand, could forgive. I still saw a future for us when the dust settled. Perhaps she'd be able to see it too, I told myself.

Until I got the letter.

If I thought the harshness of a two-sentence text was tough to bear, the reality of two pages about why we would not work, could not work, and how it had all just been some little sex fantasy and she was sorry, truly, truly sorry to disappoint, but if I were to contact her again, lawyers would be contacted.

Then to top it off was the crisp, freshly written check, with the name left blank, because she didn't even know my name, for the amount of one million dollars.

That was the price she was putting on my heart, which was now shattered into a million pieces and strewn across the floor. But the check did help me in one way. It helped me feel angry. It helped me feel the burning rage of injustice inside me.

I might be in love with her, but in writing that check, Willow made me a whore. An expensive one, but a whore nonetheless. And I was a lot of things. I never judge anyone who sells themselves, but our love was so much more than that.

I had seen enough movies and read enough books to know that I was supposed to tear up that check with indignation, that I was supposed to ride along on my moral high horse with my broke ass looking cute all the way up there.

Except I was angry and I'm not stupid. I knew a million dollars would change my life. So, I cashed it. And while I longed to go on a huge shopping spree, instead I enrolled at college for fall to study business and I let Landon know that I would finish at the club after the summer.

I didn't tell anyone else about the money, for lots of reasons, but the main one was shame. They would either think bad of me--or worse, well of me. But either way, I would use the money to change my life. I would show Willow Elizabeth Rutherford that I might be a whore, but I was a smart one, and that she was the one who had missed out.

Landon took the news well. I walked into his office, my heart pounding with anticipation. The atmosphere in the dimly lit room felt like a mix of excitement and secrecy. A worn-out leather couch sat against one wall, its cracks revealing years of use. A desk cluttered with papers and empty coffee cups stood as a silent witness to the busy nights the place had seen.

A framed poster of an exotic dancer adorned the peeling wallpaper, her sultry gaze captivating anyone who dared to look. I couldn't help but feel a strange sense of connection to her, knowing that we both embraced our sexuality in a world that tries so hard to suppress it.

The air was heavy with the scent of cigarette smoke and cheap cologne, mingling together to create an intoxicating aroma. It reminded me of the late nights I had spent dancing under neon lights, lost in the rhythm of the music and the energy of the crowd.

I glanced at the mirror hanging on the back of the door, catching a glimpse of myself. My reflection stared back at me, hair tousled from hours of teasing. Makeup slightly smudged from sweat and exertion. But in this moment, I feel more alive than ever before because, finally, I can feel an end in sight. And it's one of my choosing. I wouldn't have to settle for the future that Pearl ended up with.

I'm short and direct, but I tell Landon that I'm giving him a couple of months' notice, so I think we can end on good terms. He agrees that we can and says that he appreciates that. Unasked questions linger in the air, but I don't feel the need to volunteer any more information.

He leans forward, though, with those dreamy blues, and asks me softly, "You gonna be okay, Lola? Because if you need anything--if you're in trouble--I can help."

It's Landon's genuine concern that pushes me to tell him just a little more. "I'm going back to school. It's time. I can't do this forever. I got a chance and I just think I should take it. Try and sit that side of the desk for a change—with more clothes on." I grin and he smirks.

"You belong on either side of this desk, probably over it too on some occasions, clothing optional. But good. I am proud of you. If you need anything, you call me, okay? This place is special to me, but it isn't my only venture in town. Maybe I have a better fit for you, when the time comes."

"Maybe you do, Landon, but either way . . . I'll be sad to say goodbye to you and this place."

"Oh, I don't think you'll be gone for good. It's still one of the best-stocked bars this side of the river."

"I will pass on to Pearl your high praise." I grin as I stand, and he does too. A second passes. Do we hug, shake hands, or go for the side cheek kiss? Instead, Landon shrugs, with his soft smile, and sits back down.

"I don't like goodbyes anyway. Get out of here." I go to leave. As the door closes, Landon calls after me, "And you still gotta put on the best shows! I ain't paying you for half-assed booty shaking!" he hollers, in his best leery strip guy voice. I laugh as I head to the stage, the exit countdown on. I keep my heart in an armored box, never showing the faintest hint of just how broken it is, underneath the steel cage.

17

WILLOW

I sit alone in my apartment, surrounded by the remnants of our love that once bloomed. The air is heavy with sadness and neglect, mirroring the state of my heart. Each corner seems to hold memories of laughter and joy that have faded away.

The walls, once painted with vibrant colors, now bear the marks of weariness. It's as if they too have absorbed the weight of my tears and silently echo my pain. Dusty shelves display trinkets that we collected together, each serving as a painful reminder of what we have lost. Or of what I have lost.

A sense of emptiness pervades every inch of

this place. The couch where we cuddled feels cold and unwelcoming, like a stranger I no longer recognize. It's hard to believe that just weeks ago, warmth and love filled these rooms. Now, all that remains is an overwhelming feeling of loneliness and despair.

I cry for the loss of a love that was so beautiful, yet so fragile. An impossible love. My heart aches for the touch that used to ignite sparks within me, now replaced by the icy grip of knowing that it was because of me. I did this.

The words from my letter to Lola play over and over in my head. I went hard; I was cruel. And with every word I wrote, I felt a stab in my heart. But I had wanted to make her angry. To make Lola feel rage, so she would take the money and move on. So she would build a life without me and at least one of us could be happy. Because all I could feel was misery.

My mother, who had never been in my apartment, was around every few days now. She ad hstarted to remove every remnant of Lola. Well, the ones she could see, the ones that weren't imprinted in my head. In my heart. The ones that played on a loop every single day.

I'd lost weight and my skin looked grey, and my

hair seemed greasy no matter how much I washed it. And as often as my mother tried to get me all nice and pretty, it never really looked right.

Work is the only place I can shine, the only thing that matters because I've given up everything else. I can't fail now.

But I find myself constantly thinking about Lola, stalking her almost, in my head. Running through her day, her routine, wondering if anything has changed. Maybe she quit her job, maybe she moved, maybe, maybe, maybe. I have no idea and no right at all to know. This is my punishment for my selfishness.

I can see the panic start to form in my mother. The worry that grows and grows. I have never shown vulnerability and have never let sadness show. But now I live in it. I let it take over my entire being. I know it must be hard for her to watch-- hard for her to see me lose myself, knowing that she is very much responsible.

I won't go up to the house. Not for any other reason than I don't want to see my father. He has always disappointed me, but that night, when he had the chance to step in, to say he would love me even though I was gay and that of course I would always be his daughter . . . he didn't. For me, that was the end of our relationship. I will be civil to him, but the tolerance is gone and my need to have his approval has disappeared. As far as I'm concerned, he showed me what mattered: my name, but not my happiness.

"You have to forgive him at some point, Willow," my mom says softly when I put his birthday invite in the trash.

I look straight at her. "Would you? Would you forgive Pawpaw if he did that to you? Would you forgive Grandma, for that matter?" My voice is laced with venom--I can hear it. I see her physically recoil and I don't even feel bad. All I feel is nothingness.

Sitting in my small, dimly lit cubicle, I am engulfed in a whirlwind of emotions. My heart feels heavy, burdened by sadness and longing. The remnants of our once-beautiful relationship still linger in my head, reminding me of what we had and what is now lost.

I stare at my phone, debating whether to call her or nota. It's been weeks since we broke up, but the pain is still as fresh as if it happened yesterday.

Memories flood my mind like waves crashing against the shore, leaving behind fragments of love and happiness that have been shattered.

My fingers tremble as I pick up the phone, hesitating for a moment before dialing Lola's number. A part of me hopes she'll answer, hoping I can hear her voice one more time. Maybe she will understand the ache inside my chest and offer some solace. Maybe even a glimmer of hope. But then reality sets in. The truth is, calling Lola won't fix anything. I go to end the call quickly but not before I hear the automated message, "*Number no longer in service.*"

And it is like Willow actually answered, telling me what I already know. I don't deserve to seek solace from her; I should be left to feel like this. Because I broke us, I broke her, and I have to live with it. Except I just have to see her. I have to know that she's okay. So I make my decision. Tonight I will go to the club, just to check on her. It'll be for her, completely.

But even in my head it is half-hearted. It's not for her at all. It is all for me.

I sit in front of the mirror, staring at my reflection as I apply my makeup. Tonight is the night I'll see her again. As I carefully swipe on some mascara, I can't help but feel a sense of emptiness within me. All I see in my reflection is a clown painting on a smile.

It was our place, where we met, our little sanctuary. A place where we could escape from the world and just be ourselves. But now it feels like everything has changed.

I try to push away the thoughts that linger in my mind, reminding myself that tonight is about finding closure. But no matter how hard I try, the pain still lingers deep within my chest. Every stroke of lipstick reminds me of the passionate kisses we shared, while every swipe of the brush through my hair brings back memories of her gentle touch.

I take a deep breath and remind myself that tonight is not about winning Lola back. It's about accepting that she's moved on and finding the strength to do the same. But as I slip into my favorite dress, I can't help but wonder if I'll ever find someone who will love me the way she did. And what kind of person I am, to have let her go.

18

LOLA

I walk into the back room of the strip club, feeling a mix of excitement and nerves. The space is dimly lit, with a row of mirrors lining one wall. I find an empty chair in front of one mirror and take a deep breath.

I carefully unpacked my bag, laying out the tools of my trade. A palette of vibrant makeup brushes waiting to be used like magic wands. Jars of glittery eyeshadow that beckon me. I start with a clean canvas, applying foundation first, to even out my complexion. As I blend it in, I imagine the flawless mask I'll wear tonight.

Next comes the transformation of my eyes. With each stroke of eyeliner, my gaze becomes more captivating, designed to draw people in like moths to a flame. Layers of mascara coat my lashes, adding a touch of allure and mystery. Eyeshadow colors dance across my lids, accentuating their natural beauty.

A hint of blush adds a youthful flush to my cheeks, while lipstick adorns my lips in bold hues. Each shade represents a different facet of myself—confident reds, playful pinks, or seductive plums. Choosing the right one is always an important decision because it sets the tone.

Next, I slip into my outfit for the evening—a dance set that hugs my curves in all the right places. As I adjust the straps and make sure everything sits comfortably, I can't help but admire how confident and alluring I look.

I take a moment to stretch and warm up my body. Dancing takes strength and flexibility, so it's important to limber up beforehand. I do some simple stretches, feel my muscles loosen, and prepare myself mentally for what's to come.

I straighten my posture, reminding myself to exude confidence and grace as I move.

"Lola, sweetie." Pearl pokes her head around the door frame and gives me the eyes of someone who has something to say but doesn't want to say it.

"Yes?"

"I thought you would want to know that *she's* here. We didn't know if we should turn her away or not, but in the end, we thought it should be up to you."

I feel ice run through me, my heart pounding and a little tremble in my fingers, which I instantly hide. I never drop my smile, not even for a second. I turn back to Pearl. "Who is here?" I say, with a shrug and a smirk. #

Pearl winks back at me. "Knock em dead. All of them."

Willow sits, arms resting on the edge of the bar, savoring the last drops of her bourbon as the stage lights up. The first chord strikes out . . . and there I am. Well, what did she expect?

"*Told me, told me . . .*" My body has an almost iridescent glow under the spotlight. All hint of summer has left my skin and I'm paler than usual. I'm wearing black satin that doesn't just rest against my curves, it enhances them--making them even more seductive. Long eyelashes, thickened with jet-black mascara and lined in deep kohl, frame my eyes. My lips are a deep cherry-red pout, and they press against the old-fashioned steel as I lip-sync into the microphone. My blue eyes sparkle boldly.

"You have been wasting time . . . on the other side." Each whispered lyric is delivered straight to Willow. I wonder if she can remember how it feels to have my words whisper on her skin--my gasps, my moans. My hips sway softly as the satin brushes against my thighs. My heel taps in time to the music, stilettos so high that they make me several inches taller. My legs shimmer from the hosiery catching the light, and I can feel the snap of my garter belt straps against my skin with every move I make.

"Didn't think about it when you let me down . . ." My body turns to the side as the bass begins. The lights pulse to the rhythm and I feel the heat of them on my skin as I start to dance. My hands stretch up, my fingers entwining to make the black silky satin pull tight across my chest.

"Chase me, Chase me." The shadows move on either side of me. One at my front, one at my back. Tall, oiled beauties in fitted black panties and

nothing more. The lights stay focused on me, but their presence makes me tingle with anticipation. My body is sandwiched between two girls who know what they want. Their attention heightens the pulse of arousal through me, eyes on me, breath against my neck, fingers on my skin. "*Is it feeding all your fears?*"

My head tips back and I feel the press of her lips against my pulse, teething grazing along my neck, sending shivers down my spine. Fingers reach forward to lightly sweep the thin straps from my shoulders, tracing down my arms as I feel the satin slip from my skin. It drops in a cascade of silk, pooling at my stilettos. Leaving my breasts bare and my body on display "*Oh . . . I know what you're about to say . . .*"

She drops to her knees behind me and I feel the trace of her chin down my spine. Lips never leave my skin until I feel her teeth pull at my lacy panties and the fabric tightens against my pussy at the front. At the same time, kisses pepper my collarbone, painting my skin with desire. I feel her panties against me as my body aches for her, and I gasp . . . "*Bet you wanna love me now . . .*"

Her thumbs brush over my ankle bones, then her palms glide up my stockings. Fingers fanning as they reach my thighs, inching higher as her teeth release my panties, making a snap against my skin. From the front, hungry lips travel further down my body. Placing a kiss directly between my breasts, she sticks out her tongue and paints a line of lust straight down to my navel as she, too, sinks to her knees for me.

I turn on my heels to face forward. Both of their hands inch higher. Skimming the lace tops of my stockings, finger pads on silky flesh before reaching the hem of black lace that rests against my hips.

The moment they find it, my eyes meet Willow's. She knows me so well. She will notice the flush of arousal on my chest and the tremble in my thighs . . . *"But I'll keep that between you and I . . ."*

My hand grips the pole as the women's fingers hook, and lace drags down my thighs. It clings to my pussy . . . but their want is greater, so it peels away from me. They lower my panties all the way down to my ankles. I feel the spotlight bathe my nakedness, lighting me up. Every inch of me is on display . . . bold and beautiful. *"Bet you wanna love me now."*

I look straight at Willow to see tears streak

19

WILLOW

I stumble out of the club and retch in the lot, throwing up whatever I ate before. I want to get away as soon as possible, but my legs are weak and my head is spinning. Instead, I sit down on the curb. Tears and snot stream down my face. It was a slap and I deserve it. I deserve that sting, to feel how much Lola doesn't need me.

She looked so beautiful and I had been so lucky, so fucking lucky. My entire body shakes with sobs as I suddenly feel a hand on my back. I look up, startled, to see the owner of the club. I wipe my face with my coat and try to stand.

"Sorry, I'll be going," I say. "I didn't mean to cause an issue."

He looks at me with kind eyes and seems to weigh his next words carefully.

"You're not causing an issue. I just . . . I know what you saw. But it is a show, and Lola, well, she's the best there is. They wrote songs about her, you know, the greatest showgirl I have. Well, had."

"Had?" I ask softly, interest piqued, desperate for any information I can get about her. He considers for a moment longer, then sits down beside me on the curb.

"I know who you are, Ms. Rutherford," he says matter-of-factly, and I like him for his directness. "I understand the dilemma because I've felt it myself. I have businesses all across town and I run in some circles that don't approve of this place. But you know what—I love it here. This place is my favorite thing that I own. Don't ask me why. My shrink is working on that shit. But anyway, the point is, people have opinions. But they also still shake my hand. Still like my cash. My friends still hang out with me. My sister rolls her eyes but still loves me. Do you get what I'm saying? Sometimes it is hard to hold onto the things we love because of what others think, but after the dust settles, they adapt. But if you let go of what you love, that shit can be gone. Forever." He hands me a tissue from his pocket and I wipe my cheek.

"I think the one I love is gone. Forever."

He stands up beside me slowly. "Nah, she ain't. Like I said, a showgirl through and through. Lola is the ultimate professional. The show goes on even when her heart is broken, and believe me, it is. She is tough, Lola. She has to be. She had a rough start to life and has had to fight hard for everything she has."

"And yes, she is leaving," he says. "Going back to school. Seems like someone has made an impression on her, a good one. One that showed her how to love herself, maybe."

I nod as Landon starts to walk away. Nothing more is said because nothing more needs to be said. I know what Landon is saying, what he thinks. And as I stare out across the lot, I can't help but think that he is completely right.

I stand nervously outside my father's massive office, clutching the hem of my dress. It has been years since I've been here and a very long time since we've last spoken with anything other than civility. Our relationship is like a fragile glass sculpture, ready to shatter with a single wrong move.

Taking a deep breath, I gather the courage to knock on the towering wooden door. Finally he calls me in, his voice cold and distant.

Stepping into the opulent space, I can't help but feel out of place. Expensive artwork adorns the walls, while polished mahogany furniture fills the room. My father sits behind an imposing desk, engrossed in paperwork.

I approach him cautiously, fidgeting with my fingers. "Daddy," I begin hesitantly, trying to keep my emotions in check. "I need your help."

His gaze darts up from his work, clearly surprised. "What do you need, Willow?"

"I need you to make it all okay, Daddy. I don't know . . . I don't know how anymore. I don't know what to do. Please, please help me."

My father has longed for me to be the little girl that turned to him for help. He has wanted to be the man I used to put on the pedestal. Maybe it's my show of emotion, my plea for his help, and my obvious desperation--or maybe it's because he truly does love me and wants me to be happy. But I see the relief in his face as he nods, looking me straight in the eye. "I will fix it."

And for the first time in weeks I can finally breathe.

It takes time, patience, and perseverance. My mother was the first obstacle but when Daddy told her that this was going to happen with the voice he usually saved for running his office, she knew better than to do anything other than nod.

It gave her a project at least. Somewhere she could focus her time and her energy. Turning her daughter into the ideal political candidate who was openly homosexual. No easy task, but one that time, money, and tenacity could address. And we had all of those things in ample supply.

Because if I make it in politics, I can make changes that will revolutionise things for women, and for all LGBTQ people.

I don't contact Lola. Not yet. I need to do this first. I need to be who I am. It's time for me to own my mistakes and to love myself for the woman I am—a strong, willful, intelligent woman who is also attracted to women.

I'm not sure if Lola will see my campaign announcement. I don't get the impression she follows politics much, but who knows?

The gay angle isn't going to be worked in, not as a part of my campaign platform, anyway--but it won't be hidden, either. Not a secret. I want the question people ask not to be about whether I am gay. Rather, will I do my job well, and represent you as a citizen of this great state? And maybe one day, even the country?

The people will decide.

"Ladies and gentlemen, thank you all for gathering here today at the steps of the Justice Department. It is with great pride and excitement that I stand before you to announce my candidacy for representative of this great district. This moment marks a significant milestone in my life, as I embark on my journey to serve and represent the people." I take a deep breath.

"I am deeply committed to making positive changes within our community by fighting for justice and equality for all. Throughout my career, I have witnessed the struggles faced by many individuals and families who are desperate for change. Today, I pledge to be their voice, their advocate, and their champion." There is a little cheer from the small crowd in front of me that has gathered. I can see my mother beaming from the side.

"I believe in the power of unity and collaboration. Together, we can create a society where everyone has equal opportunities, regardless of their background or circumstances. We must work toward ensuring affordable healthcare, quality education, and job security for every individual who is striving to build a better future." My father is mouthing along with me. I can see the pride in his face as I deliver the words as we've practiced for the public stage.

Politics will always be his first love and I can see that in following him into that, it has become entirely irrelevant to him that I am gay.

A suitable husband is no longer the goal. A Rutherford in the White House is the goal, whether it is him or me.

"My campaign will focus on transparency, accountability, and integrity. It's time to restore faith in our political system and to regain the trust of the people we aim to serve. As your representative, I promise to listen to your concerns, engage in open dialogue, and to make decisions that truly reflect the needs and aspirations of our diverse population."

"I understand that running for office comes with immense responsibility..."

And then suddenly I see her. Lola.

She shines like a beacon. Lola is wearing a very conservative dark red Gucci shift dress and heels. The whole ensemble looks like it could have come from my own wardrobe. Her dark hair is glossy and immaculate, and swept neatly into an updo. Her makeup is understated. Lola looks classy, like a grown up version of the Lola I knew. Surprisingly, it suits her. Lola looks as beautiful as ever.

She is looking up at me, listening to me, with her navy blue eyes sparkling. I want to jump off the podium and straight into her arms.

"*Finish your speech first,*" she mouths, and I continue speaking as though nothing has happened. If there is one thing I have learned from Lola, it is that the show must go on. Nodding to her, I feel renewed energy as I storm through my closing statement, delivering it with the hope and optimism for a future that I feel deep within me as Lola looks up at me. My beautiful Lola, who is so many things, but never a showgirl to me.

EPILOGUE PART 1
LOLA- 15 YEARS LATER

The scent of seduction lingers in the air. The stage gleams, but this is no cheap club. The mirrors are polished to reflect angles, to give glimpses of secret delights.

But tonight--for one night only--Lola is back, for a private function. This time, only Willow and I will be here.

I dealt with some nerves as I dressed, with the realization that years had passed and my body didn't look, feel, and move the way it once did. But there was also excitement running through my veins about being back. Having this feeling one more time.

And for a very special cause. Performing for Willow will always be my favorite.

I step forward, my skyscraper black stilettos clicking across the mirrored floor. My black pants are tailored to perfection. I doubt anything else could make my ass look this good ... riding the curve of my peachy flesh and then cutting in to follow my long legs. My fingers snap softly in time to the beat.

My jacket is buttoned to my chest, creating a wide V that begins at the valley between the swell of my breasts and runs up to my shoulders. My hair is pulled up into a high, perfect ponytail. Dark kohl is swept into cat-eye flicks that exaggerate the sparkle of my blue eyes. Finally, a seductive smear of scarlet goes across my lips.

I reach the edge of the stage and turn to the side, my figure defined by the crisp edge of my fitted suit. I look up under thick lashes, my eyes filled with invitation. My curves are accentuated as I make my way down with a sleek side step, hips rolling to the long, slow throb of the bass. My heel finds the club floor and I turn to face her.

I step forward with a confident stride. "I would leave with me tonight . . ." I whisper under my breath as I reach Willow. My palm rests against her cheek, guiding her gaze up to meet mine, as I slowly drag my thumb over her deliciously pouted lips. "Ladies first, baby, I insist..."

As I feel the tingles of her breath against my skin... I slip away. My hand rises and my fingernails trace a straight line down my chest, unhooking the button with a swift flick as my shoulders give a slow, sensual roll. My blazer falls, discarded, and the spotlight dips to focus on the crumpled heap of clothing before sweeping up my body like a voyeuristic gaze.

I invade Willow's space, my head dipping so that my lips glance against her earlobe. With a low sensual whisper, I say, "I never would have left you alone." Standing in front of her, I drop my fingers to my hips, to tease the fabric of my pants. I peel them down, inch by inch, and my ass sways. I make slow, seductive circles as the clothing rides down over my curves. My tiny panties are black and silky. Their only purpose is to hold the cash.

My pants drop to my ankles and I step out of them. I'm balanced on my stilettos, wearing just the slip of string. It invites Willow's gaze, and her hungry, amber eyes feast on my body.

"I could be a better boyfriend than him..." I sing to her along with the song, as my knees rise up... left... then right... to straddle her lap. My thighs spread and my hips dip, offering a long slow drag of my sex against her thighs.

As my head drops to pepper kisses along her jaw, there is a slow scrape of my teeth as I feel the heat building between us. "Congratulations, Madame Vice President."

I smile and she smiles back. I'm so proud of her, and I know she is proud of herself. She should be.

Then I pull her to me, feeling her kiss me back with the dizzying heat only she possesses.

Everything has changed for us, but at the same time, nothing has.

EPILOGUE PART 2
WILLOW

As I entered the opulent office bathed in natural light, my attention was immediately drawn to her – my strikingly gorgeous brunette wife who effortlessly commanded the room.

It no longer matters that she never had a surname, now she is Mrs. Lola Rutherford and she has never looked back.

The luxurious space seemed to revolve around her, as if the very essence of elegance and professionalism emanated from her presence.

Her glossy dark hair is professionally done these days and it cascaded down her back in loose waves, framing a face adorned with a smattering of freckles that only enhanced her captivating charm.

Lola is as beautiful as she ever has been, only these days she has a designer wardrobe and a hairstylist and beauty consultant on speed dial. (and she loves these perks, by the way.)

Her navy blue eyes sparkled with intelligence and determination, reflecting the ambient light that danced through the expansive windows. The subtle curve of her lips suggested both confidence and approachability, creating an aura that beckoned you to engage in conversation.

Seated at an impeccably organized desk, she epitomized efficiency and grace amid her multitasking. A sleek MacBook occupied the center stage, its silver glow complementing the warm tones of the mahogany furnishings. With one hand skillfully navigating the keyboard, and the other holding a sleek smartphone pressed to her ear, she effortlessly balanced a myriad of responsibilities.

As her voice resonated through the airwaves of the room, it carried a blend of authority and friendliness. The conversation flowed seamlessly, a testament to her adept communication skills. Meanwhile, her fingers danced across the keyboard, effortlessly toggling between applications on the Mac screen.

My Lola hasn't grown, she has flourished. Blossomed into the flower I knew she could be. I hated the pain I caused her, but what she did in the aftermath showed exactly the woman I have always known she was. Strong, clever, fierce, and unstoppable.

Supporting me in my political career as a wife would have been one thing, but she has gone beyond that and is in every way my partner- I could not have made it this far without her. She has gone to school and studied business and politics, she is the biggest asset to my team and the person I trust more than any other.

Landon helped her get started before she became part of my team.

He didn't make it easy for her. He put her to work in his various businesses. He pushed all kinds of things her way and forced her to learn, change, adapt, and grow. But boy did she grow. More than I think even he could have imagined, doubling his worth in the first year. So this fancy, opulent downtown office and position at the top of my team? She earned every single inch of it.

She looked up from her screen and gave me

the warmest of smiles, she glowed with happiness and contentment, and that smile, it felt like home to me.

My family tried not to be dazzled by her, but it didn't last long. My mother held out the longest but even she couldn't resist Lola's undeniable charm. And Lola wasn't even actively trying, she didn't try to win her over or pretend to be anyone other than who she was. Warm, kind, funny, and genuine. Before I knew it she was getting more calls than I was, "Lola which color shirt would pair best with these pants for the Manatee Gala?"

It took Lola some time to decide that I was her future, which was completely understandable, I had hurt her, my family had hurt her and she didn't want to fit into a world where people and feelings were so dispensable. But the truth was that that world is part of me. I could learn from it, change, and be different. But it was that world that had shaped me and by denying that and pushing it away only served me to make the same mistakes again. So in time, Lola accepted that world too, its matching pants and all.

My political career has flown since my parents got on board with the challenge of selling me as an openly homosexual candidate.

I could feel aggrieved at the way my family behaved years ago, at the restrictions that were put on my life and the cloying homophobia and classist attitude that surrounded me. I did feel aggrieved, for a time. I didn't want their support or anything to do with them.

But as the pain faded, I realized I could use my position as a Rutherford. For my benefit. Mine and hopefully Lola's and hopefully also to the benefit of the women of the US and maybe even the rest of the world too.

Sure I had spent my twenties already dabbling in politics, as a Rutherford, what else did I know? It was in my blood. But it took one morning waking up next to Lola and just believing. With her at my side I suddenly believed I could change the world and the ambition to make it to the very highest office began burning deep within me.

We could do it together. I knew we could.

So, I used my name and my parents' power to get me as far as they could.

Their next challenge was how to spin Lola the stripper as my new wife. But, it is amazing what a good team can do. Lola the 'dancer with the heart of gold' was only a very minor scandal early in my career, we got out ahead of things and told the story on our own terms. We sold the narrative we wanted to tell the people and it is amazing how hard it then became for my opponents to pull me down.

And then you put Lola in a designer pantsuit and get her a professional blow-dry and make up and she *looks* the part. She gives one of her dazzling Lola smiles and wins everyone over. Lola, it turns out, wasn't a tough sell to the people after all.

Now, nobody can barely remember anything about Lola before she was Mrs. Rutherford. Nobody remembers Lola the stripper. They might think for a second that they do, but Lola's beauty is now so classic and her wardrobe so conservative, that even the men she has danced for, they think it must have been another Lola, that sexy creature of the night who used to take their dollars and make them feel wanted in the darkness of the club.

It turns out the US is more than ready for the power lesbians anyway if my recent progression to Vice President tells you anything.

People love Lola. That hasn't changed. The most successful presidents in history had the strongest and most charming wives and I aim to continue that tradition.

I want to be the first female president of the United States hopefully by the time I am 50. We are long overdue a woman in the most powerful position in the world and I intend it to be me.

We had three children.

Yes! Three!

Sophia, Lily and Rose. Our beautiful girls. Lola carried and gave birth to each of them. Every day I am in awe of her for what she went through with pregnancy and birth. We chose to use Landon as the sperm donor, although we kept his identity hidden, we wanted our girls to know where they came from genetically and he was happy to always be there for them.

Every day when I look at their beautiful smiles it reminds me of everything I am fighting for. I am fighting to make our wonderful country a better place for them and every other little girl in America to grow up in. And that has to be the most valiant fight of all.

I lie in bed with Lola late in the morning, something I have never really adapted to. I spend most of the time with my eyes open, watching the light dance along the curtains. Feeling her move, and watching her body so beautiful in the morning light. Relaxed and at ease.

I slowly wrap my hands around her and pull her close, giving her a soft squeeze and I feel her shiver and kiss me back in a dreamy state of need.

I roll on top of her and rock my body against hers. Our bodies pressed together so tightly they kiss all over.

I slide my knee between her thighs to press against her clitoris, my hands moving around to her ass.

She lets out a gasp and a moan as I pull her where I want her.

My nails dig into her ass cheeks. She gasps into my mouth as she grinds on my thigh.

I kiss her and I push my tongue into her mouth and swirl it deeply. She feels so wet against my thigh.

I move her faster knowing she will be getting close. She loves having me on top of her like this.

She clings to me and kisses me, urgently.

She slides so easily now, my thigh so wet with her desire.

I reach behind her and get her favorite stainless steel anal plug. I roll us both onto our sides and I run it up her inner thigh from behind her and swirl it all around her pussy, it's so cold as she makes it so wet. I make sure it is plenty wet from her arousal before I push it to tease her anus. She moans loudly and I smile. I enjoy giving her this, her favorite toy while she is still half asleep.

Our lust for one another has remained as strong as it was at the start. Sure with the ebbs and flows of life, desire has followed and there have been periods of time where sex hasn't been a high priority for us. But we make sure to bring things back to where they started when the storms finally pass. These lazy mornings in bed together always do it for me. We don't get them often as my job places huge demands on me. But, when we do, when it is just us and I know our nanny has gotten the children up and out, I feel relaxed and turned on by Lola's beauty in the morning light again. As though the clock has turned back the years and we are back in my apartment when we barely knew each other.

Our mouths are still locked together as I tease with my fingers first and then slowly push the toy into her ass. I feel her spread for my fingers and then the toy slides in almost easily.

I can hear her moan again and she purrs as it

enters her. I grip her ass again and push her back onto her back as I work her pussy against my thigh.

She wraps herself around me, Clinging to me and softly whimpering and moaning as I hold her tight and grind my thigh against her clitoris. She has such sweet purrs and deep moans. The cheeks of her ass feels so good in my hands, her pussy feels so good against my thigh, so desperate for every touch.

I don't give her ass enough attention sometimes and it's so delicious to feel it in my hands.

I take my mouth from hers and move my lips to take her nipple in. I draw it in and suck. I want to taste every part of her.

I know this will take her to the edge as I tease her nipple with my teeth. She clings harder to me, grinding her clitoris against any part of me that she can.

"You need to come for me, baby girl?"

"Yes," she whimpers.

"Ok, baby. Come for me, now."

I clamp down on her nipple and grip her ass hard as I pin her down with my body and press my hips into her.

She moans loudly as her orgasm overtakes her

and I feel a sweet hot gush against the very top of my thigh. I keep my hands on her ass, kissing up her quivering body, her neck to her throat to her lips and then I hold her there against me and I can feel her pulse race against my lips. Her heart is beating so very fast, her body is trembling against mine but I just hold her tighter. She kisses my lips. Pressing so much against them, holding us locked in the tightest of embraces, our bodies are woven, intertwined, the tightest grip of lovers, wet with sweat, need, and desire for each other.

"That's it, baby girl, I've got you," I whisper as she lies against me. I don't loosen my hold, I hold her so tight as her eyes start to close and her body relaxes in my arms.

"I've always got you."

Her mouth is right against mine, kissing and breathing together, needing her air as much as she needs mine. I share it with her, and with every kiss I give her more.

Her eyes flicker open as I release my grip on her and we relax into our luxury sheets.

I know she is my forever, and I think I always knew it. Deep down inside.

I hope she knows it too.

Everything has changed for us, but at the same time, nothing has.

I smile at her and kiss her.

"I love you, Mrs. Rutherford."

She smiles back, as dazzling as she ever was and then she nuzzles her face into my neck.

I feel a rush of love and gratitude for Lola.

My Lola.

My forever and always.

THANK YOU FOR READING

As you probably know by now, if you have read my other books, I love an unlikely couple from different worlds, where in the end, love conquers all.

In the Senator's Daughter, I wanted to capture the seductive charm that a woman like Lola holds and I hope I managed that well.

I guess we all know a 'Lola'. A woman who is charming, beautiful and oozing sexuality.

In Willow, we have the typical trappings of someone who has grown up as she has. She doesn't navigate them perfectly, but I hope in the end, she redeems herself.

I adored writing both of these strong women

FREE BOOK

Pick up my book, Summer Love for FREE when you sign up to my mailing list.

On a beach in France, Summer crashes into Max's life and changes everything. This is a hot and heady summer romance. https://BookHip.com/MFPGZAX

My mailing list is the best place to be the first to find out about new releases, Free books, special offers and price drops. You'll also find out a bit about my life and the inspiration behind the stories and the characters. Oh, and you'll love Summer Love. :)

ALSO BY MARGAUX FOX

If you liked this book, please do check out the next in the series:

Lesbian sensation, Raven Ramsay finds herself at a crossroads in her life. What is there for her beyond this fame that she has? She is holding onto the last remnants of her music career on a Sapphic Women's only cruise. She finds herself drawn to the one woman on the cruise who doesn't know who she is. What will

Printed in Great Britain
by Amazon